DIMI OF TH

*Deliciously Wicked
Temptation Unveiled*

Jenika Snow

EROTIC ROMANCE

Siren Publishing, Inc.
www.SirenPublishing.com

A SIREN PUBLISHING BOOK
IMPRINT: Erotic Romance

DIMI OF THE SEVEN MOONS
Deliciously Wicked
Temptation Unveiled
Copyright © 2010 by Jenika Snow

ISBN-10: 1-61034-044-2
ISBN-13: 978-1-61034-044-1

First Printing: October 2010

Cover design by Jinger Heaston
All cover art and logo copyright © 2010 by Siren Publishing, Inc.

ALL RIGHTS RESERVED: This literary work may not be reproduced or transmitted in any form or by any means, including electronic or photographic reproduction, in whole or in part, without express written permission.

All characters and events in this book are fictitious. Any resemblance to actual persons living or dead is strictly coincidental.

Printed in the U.S.A.

PUBLISHER
Siren Publishing, Inc.
www.SirenPublishing.com

DEDICATIONS

Deliciously Wicked

To everyone who supported me. Without you guys I wouldn't have gone through with my dream.

Temptation Unveiled

I would like to thank everyone who helped bring this book to life. Without everyone from Siren Publishing who worked so diligently to make this book what it is, it wouldn't be a reality. I also want to thank the readers, because without you guys reading my stories, I wouldn't have any desire to write more. Thank you!

SIREN PUBLISHING *Classic*

DELICIOUSLY WICKED

Dimi of the Seven Moons

Jenika Snow

DELICIOUSLY WICKED

Dimi of the Seven Moons 1

JENIKA SNOW
Copyright © 2010

Chapter One

Squatting on all fours, Mena rummaged under her bed. "Kitty, have you seen my jeans?" Blindly reaching under her bed, she pulled stuff out and tossed it aside.

"Which ones are you talking about?" Kitty said through a mouthful of mashed-up banana.

Mena gave up looking under the bed and sat with her legs crossed on the floor. Staring at Kitty, she couldn't help but feel a little bit envious of her best friend and roommate.

Kitty and Mena met in high school and since then had been inseparable. They became roommates in college and after graduating, nothing changed. Mena was more of the strong-willed, opinionated type. Kitty's personality fell more towards the shy and passive side.

Kitty and Mena were total opposites when it came to looks as well. Kitty's hair fell in wheat-colored waves down her back—her eyes the clearest color of blue. Along with her perfect girl next door looks, Kitty was also a glorified virgin.

Mena always thought herself more on the average side with her "voluptuous" body, as she liked to say, shoulder-length, stick-straight black hair and gray eyes.

Kitty, being so soft hearted, threw compliments out like they were going out of style. Whenever Mena felt down, Kitty would say, "Mena, babe, you are beautiful with killer curves, great tits, gorgeous black, silky hair, and beautiful gray eyes that make me think of stormy afternoons."

Looking at Kitty, she got off the floor and headed over to her dresser. "You know, my favorite ones that make my thighs look killer and my ass awesome!"

"Mena, hun, you are hot shit, and you know any guy would be lucky to tap that ass!" Moving over to the bed, Kitty lay on her belly and finished eating her banana. "All of your jeans make you look good. I'm jealous of your curves!"

"Well tonight I have that date I told you about, and I want to look good."

Tossing the banana peel in the trash, Kitty switched to her back and stared at the ceiling. "Oh, yeah, the blind date with *Dick*, right?" Looking over at Mena, Kitty gave her a wicked grin.

"Yeah, the blind date with *Dick*. So, do you know where they are?"

"No, I don't, but is he picking you up here? Where are you guys eating?"

Bent over, Mena pulled her clothes out of her dresser. "I told him I would meet him at the restaurant. Just seems kind of weird having a blind date pick me up at the house, doesn't it?" Mena looked over her shoulder and crinkled her nose.

"Yeah, I guess that is kind of weird, but as soon as the date's over, call me!" Getting off the bed, Kitty headed to the door.

"Ah ha, I found them." Mena looked at Kitty with a huge smile on her face.

"You're crazy. Have fun tonight!"

* * * *

Pulling into her driveway with a frown on her face, Mena turned off her car and sat there staring off into space. Finally climbing out of her car, she shut the door and stared up into the starry night sky.

No more blind dates, Mena! Maybe you should just give up on men altogether!

She let out a sigh and pulled herself away from the car. She walked to the front door, dreading telling Kitty about the date. She knew Kitty would get a kick out of the whole thing and laugh her ass off.

Before she could even reach for the handle, Kitty flung the door open with a huge smile on her face. "Well, tell me, tell me! I have been waiting to hear the juiciness."

"Damn, Kitty, let me get in the door first. You're just going laugh anyway." Mena moved past the smiling Kitty and headed into the kitchen.

"Oh man, this one of those dates where you have to come home and have a beer, isn't it?" Kitty said, right on Mena's heels.

Throwing her purse on the counter, Mena headed over to the fridge and pulled out a beer. "Well, where to begin, where to begin?" Opening her beer, Mena propped her hip on the counter and stared at Kitty. "Promise not to laugh?"

"It's that bad, huh? Okay, I promise!"

Taking a swig of her beer, Mena smirked inwardly. "Okay, well I got there, and I saw him waiting outside like planned. He was cute, I guess kind of balding, but I didn't really care. He had manners, held the door open for me, pulled the chair out for me, you know, really nice stuff." Blowing out some breath, she continued, "So we ordered our food and everything, and all of the sudden he starts asking me about my dental history. I mean, I didn't think too much about it since he is a dentist and all, but then after dinner he scooted his chair next to me and asked me to open my mouth so he could look at my teeth. Kit, I was so stunned I actually opened my mouth." Glancing up at

Kitty, she saw her friend holding in her laughter. "Oh, go ahead and let it out."

"Holy shit, that is so funny! That date tops all of my horrible ones put together, Mena!" Kitty threw her head back and laughed so hard she wiped away the tears under her eyes. "I'm sorry, Mena. I don't mean to laugh at you. I just can't believe there are actually people like that out there. Okay, I can believe it, but I can't believe you got stuck with one."

Going to the fridge, Kitty grabbed a beer, too, and popped the top on it. She took a long drink. "You'll find that perfect guy for you, Mena, when the time's right. You still have me." Smiling at Mena, Kitty threw her arms around her friend in a big bear hug.

Sighing, Mena hugged Kitty back. "I guess it is kind of funny. It just sucks that I have to be the other party involved in the story."

"You know, Mena, I have told you my fair share of horror dates, and if I recall correctly, you laughed your ass off at me." Gulping down the rest of her beer, Kitty walked to the trash, threw it away, and leaned against the wall.

"Yeah, you're right. You have told me some horrid ones." Smiling to herself, she finished her beer and said her goodnights to Kitty. Heading toward the bathroom, she washed up before she turned in for the night.

Chapter Two

"Mena? Hey, Mena, wake up!"

Rolling onto her back, Mena slowly opened her eyes and waited for them to focus in the darkness. "Kitty? What's wrong?" Mena said through a gravelly voice. Looking at her clock, she saw that it was the middle of the night.

Whispering, Kitty moved closer. "I don't know. It's probably nothing, but I thought I heard something in the backyard."

"What do you mean, you thought you heard something? It's nothing, probably an animal or something. Go back to bed!" She rolled back over and closed her eyes.

Whoosh, whoosh, whoosh. Turning back over and knitting her eyebrows over her eyes, Mena stared at Kitty. "What the hell? Is that what you heard?"

"Yeah, with a lot of clicking noises, too. Do you think someone is trying to break in? Should we call the police?" Kitty's voice rose as she began to panic.

"No, calm down. It's probably an animal or something." Throwing the covers off, Mena padded over to the window, pulled the curtain aside slightly, and peered out. "I don't see anything."

Whoosh, whoosh, whoosh. Turning wide eyes to Kitty, she grabbed her robe and headed for the door.

"Where are you going? Do not tell me you're going outside!" Kitty looked at her, shocked.

"I have to find out what the hell is making that noise. What if it is some kids or something, and they're destroying shit?"

"Okay, hold on, I'm coming with you." Kitty ran to her room, grabbed her robe, and met Mena at the stairs. "Are you sure we shouldn't just call the police?"

Looking at Kitty with an eyebrow raised, Mena saw that she not only grabbed her robe, but also an aluminum baseball bat. "Where did you get that thing? You don't even like baseball."

"Don't look at me that way. You want to go out there unprotected? Anyway, I got it a while back. I did have my eye on a gun." Bringing the bat up to her shoulder, she cocked her hip and stared at Mena. "So, should I call the police or what? It could be some crazed lunatic out there, you know."

"And tell them what? That we hear a strange whooshing noise? They'll laugh at us." Rolling her eyes at Kitty, she headed down the stairs. "It's probably just a stray or something. Don't go thinking the worst. You're just going to freak yourself out!"

Making their way quietly down the steps, they headed to the back of the house where the noise came from. Standing in front of the back door, Mena slowly peeled the corner of the curtain away from the door and peered out the glass. Staring wide-eyed, she let her mouth drop open. "Holy shit, what the hell is that?"

"What? Should I call the police? What is it?" Kitty pushed her out of the way. Kitty's eyes went wide and she gasped. "It has to be a trick of the moonlight or something." Unlocking the door, Kitty slowly opened it. Standing shoulder to shoulder, they both stared into their backyard. What greeted them on the other side of the door looked like something straight out of a movie.

"What is it, Kitty? It looks like something out of those sci-fi flicks." The swirling circle, which seemed to be at least six feet in height, touched the ground. Inside of the circle hues of color ranged from blues to whites to greens. The colors swirled together in a clockwise motion. The same noises they had heard in the house seemed to be coming from the "thing" in front of them.

"What should we do, Mena?"

"I don't know. Maybe we're dreaming," Mena murmured. "Ow! That hurt!" She glared at her friend and absently rubbed her arm where she got pinched.

"I just wanted to see if this was a dream."

Stepping out the door, Mena made her way toward the circular whirlpool.

"Stop! We don't even know what the thing is."

Ignoring her, Mena circled the whirlpool until she stood in front of it again. "There isn't anything behind it. I could even see a blurry version of you staring at it!" she murmured as she moved to stand next to her friend.

Doing the same, Kitty walked the circumference of it and stared at Mena with her eyebrows drawn over her eyes. Mena slowly moved her hand toward it and saw Kitty's hand strike out and stop her. "Don't. We don't even know what it is, or what will happen if you do that."

"You're right. Give me the bat." She handed the bat over, watching as if in awe as Mena stuck it into the whirlpool. It made a noise that sounded like sucking and whooshing, a gross combination. They both stared ahead in astonishment. "Kitty, go see if it's coming out on the other end."

Walking behind it, she disappeared. "I can see you and part of the bat that you're holding onto, but there isn't anything back here." Walking back to Mena, she stared at her. Pulling the bat all the way out, they both examined it. "I can't see anything wrong with it. Can you?"

Attempting some humor, Kitty smiled and said, "No. It looks like a bat." The same whooshing and sucking noise greeted them when they threw the bat into the whirlpool. Stepping closer to the whirlpool, Mena looked over at Kitty. "I'm gonna try and go through it," Mena said nervously.

"Are you crazy? We don't know what's on the other side, and we sure as hell don't even know what this thing is. It could melt you, for all we know," Kitty said in disbelief.

"Melt me? It didn't do anything to the bat, and it doesn't look like it's going anywhere, so I want to see what it can do." Slowly walking up to the whirlpool-type thing, she stuck her index finger out and slowly put it into the whirlpool. Hearing the sucking noise, she snatched her hand back and looked at it. "It looks okay. It doesn't hurt or anything."

"Did it feel weird?" Kitty asked with wide eyes.

"It felt kind of like my hand fell asleep or something. My finger felt." Mena stared at her finger. "Go get a rope or something. I'm going to try and go through."

When she didn't hear a response, she looked over. Kitty's eyes were wide, fear pouring off of her.

"What?"

"No way, sticking your finger in it is one thing, but actually walking through that thing is totally different!"

"My finger is fine, and this thing is just too weird not to check out more. Anyway, if there are any problems that you see, or if you just feel uncomfortable, then pull me out."

"I feel uncomfortable with the whole situation."

They were both silent, each one waiting for some kind of response.

"I can't talk you out of it, can I?"

"Probably not, but don't worry. It'll be fine... I hope."

Mena took the offered rope and tied it tightly around her waist. She handed the loose end to Kitty, watching as she gripped it for dear life.

"Everything will be fine. I promise." Taking a deep breath, she slowly walked toward the whirlpool. Stopping right before it, she turned around and gave a small smile.

"Mena, are you sure about this? This kind of seems like a really stupid idea."

Mena smiled once again, not having a logical answer. Turning back around, she stepped through the whirlpool.

Chapter Three

She felt lightheaded, her whole body feeling as if she were floating. Darkness surrounded her, so thick it suffocated her. She tried to focus her eyes in the darkness, but it didn't make a difference. Blindly moving her hands to her waist, she felt for the rope. She breathed out a sigh of relief, thankful the rope was still tight around her waist. She didn't know what to expect, but the fear that it had slipped loose bounded into her brain.

Turning around, she took note that the whirlpool still swirled behind her. Turning in a circle, she took in her surroundings. It took some time for her eyes to fully adjust to the darkness.

This is too weird! Where the hell am I?

She looked into the sky, her brow knitting in confusion.

The first thing she noticed about the sky was the absence of stars. She turned in a small circle and her eyes slowly widened. "No, that can't be right."

Seven translucent and pale blue moons hung in the sky, lined up horizontally from biggest to smallest.

She started to hyperventilate and turned quickly to retreat back to the whirlpool. Losing her footing, she screamed as her arms swung in every direction, trying to grab something to stop her fall. Landing on her ass several feet away, she stared up at the whirlpool as the familiar sucking and whooshing noise began.

Coming from the whirlpool, a wide-eyed and heavy-breathing Kitty emerged. "Mena? Mena! Where the hell are you? I can't see a damn thing." Mena heard the panic in her voice.

"Kit, I'm fine. I just slipped and fell. It's dark, and your eyes just haven't adjusted yet. What the hell are you doing anyway? Why did you come through the whirlpool?"

"I felt the rope tug and got scared. I thought something happened to you. I wasn't really thinking. I just jumped through the damn thing."

Sitting up, she made her way over to Kitty. She reached towards Kitty, wrapping her arms around her and giving her a big hug. "I don't know where we are, but it isn't home! Look up into the sky and tell me what you see."

Kitty pulled away and looked into the sky. Mena watched her as confusion settled in to horror.

"That can't be right. My eyes must not have adjusted yet."

"No, you're seeing right. There are seven moons in the sky! Or, at least, I think that's what they are. Now last time I checked, there weren't seven moons when we looked into the sky back home."

"You know there aren't. Where the hell are we?"

"I don't know, but I want to get out of here now!" They turned in unison, Mena taking hold of Kitty's arm. They both sucked in air at what greeted them. Nothing. She turned her head towards Kitty, her mouth unable to close all the way.

"Where is it? Oh no, what's going on here! Where is it? How are we going to get home?" Kitty spoke quickly, hysteria taking hold of her voice. She sat on the ground and pulled her knees to her chest. Kitty started to cry softly, breaking Mena's heart. Mena sat next to Kitty and pulled her close.

"I know it's hard, but you have to calm down so we can figure out what's going on. Let's look at this logically for a minute. The whirlpool thing must have been a portal of some sort, and—before you say anything—I know that sounds crazy."

She stared at Kitty, pleased when she stopped crying and looked at her. Kitty wiped her eyes, threw her head back, and laughed. Mena knew this wasn't a funny situation, but she could not help but give in to the hysteria.

Kitty said, "That's the craziest thing I've ever heard! Although, given our predicament, I would have to say you're probably right on the money. That, or we are dreaming."

"Maybe we'll wake up soon, and we can laugh about it in our own kitchen without seven moons above us." Mena stared up at the sky. "Although they are rather beautiful, don't you think?"

"I guess, in a crazy sort of way. Well, I'm giving you the leader position since you seem to be the one who is the calmest, and it was your dumb idea to go through the hell hole. So what do we do first?"

"I really don't know what to do. It's really too dark, so I say we sit here until the sun rises… if there is a sun that rises here, that is. What do you think?"

"That's as good an idea as any. I don't want to be walking around in the middle of the night anyway." Kitty shivered. "Who knows what the hell is out there. At least if the sun rises, we can see what we are dealing with." Kitty lay her head on Mena's shoulder, and they sat in silence and waited.

* * * *

Mena opened her eyes, her head feeling hazy and disoriented. *Uhhh, I feel like shit! I must have fallen asleep at a bad angle.* She rubbed her eyes and then stopped. Her eyes flew open. It all came crashing back to her. The portal… the darkness… the moons, no, scratch that, the *seven* moons. A soft snore sounded, and she turned her head. Kitty lay on her side, her face serene and calm.

Oh, thank goodness Kitty's all right!

"Kitty." She shook her lightly and spoke a little louder. "Kitty! Wake up!" Kitty rolled onto her back and rubbed her eyes. "What Mena? You know I am so not an early riser," she said with a big yawn. She stopped mid yawn and flew up into a sitting position. "Oh shit. I can't believe I actually fell asleep! Are you okay?"

"I'm fine. I can't believe we fell asleep either, given the circumstances and the hard ground beneath us." Mena stood and rubbed her back, a nasty kink settling in. She helped Kitty up, both of them looking at their surroundings. The both gasped at the same time. In front of them a jungle stretched for miles. Huge trees seemed to touch the sky, the branches so thick she wondered if even the light could penetrate. She turned around, and her breath stopped. Tugging on Kitty's shoulder, she pointed ahead. "Look at this."

Her hand still outstretched, she looked at Kitty. Kitty's eyes went wide, and her mouth dropped open. Behind them, deep blue sand stretched for miles, barren of all life. Mena looked at the jungle again, then turned and looked at the desert. "What the hell, is all I have to say. What… the… hell?"

They both decided to go into the jungle, thinking they would rather take their chances with wild animals than get heat stroke and die of dehydration. Neither one of them wanted to walk on freaky-looking sand like that anyway. They realized that death could be their outcome going this route as well.

Sweat poured off of Mena in rivers, the oppressive jungle sucking the very breath out of her. They both had decided to take off their rubbers, but that didn't even seem to help. The large trees, thick branches, and leaves above them helped to keep the sun off of them, but they also made their surroundings feel like a sauna. Mena couldn't understand how it could be so humid when a dry desert sat behind them, but then again, nothing about this situation made much sense. They found a small clearing and sat down to take a breather. They both were breathing heavily from exertion, their bodies coated in sweat and aching from walking.

Mena said, "What are we going to do? I mean, we can't walk forever until we find that portal thing again. We have no food and haven't found any water yet, if there even is any. You know what the freakiest thing about this is right now? Listen." Kitty tilted her head to listen, and gave a small shrug. "Can you even hear anything? Animals? The wind? Anything?" She scrubbed her face with her hands and let out a long sigh of frustration.

"I don't want to think much on how there seems to be no sounds. If I think about it too much, I will have another meltdown." Mena saw the frustration reflected on Kitty's face as she idly picked at her clothes. "At least we wore PJ's that are appropriate for the weather."

Mena had to laugh at her comment. She had to agree that she was glad she hadn't worn long johns. "Just think, if I would have worn my long johns, my crotch would be sweating up a storm right now." Looking at Kitty, she couldn't help but laugh at her friend's crinkled up nose.

"You're nasty, Mena," she said through a smile.

After getting back up and walking farther into the jungle, Mena stopped dead in her tracks and held her hand up for Kitty to be quiet. "Listen! Can you hear that? I think it's water." Taking Kitty's arm, she walked quickly toward the sound.

Pushing bushes and branches aside, they found a glorious oasis. To the left of them, a small waterfall flowed into a small pond. A small pool of water was surrounded by trees, bushes, and flowers of every color. The waterfall climbed ten feet into the air, and they could feel the light mist coat their faces. "Oh, look how beautiful it is! Water, glorious water. Kitty, come on!" They made their way down to the pool of water. Stopping Kitty from chugging down a handful of water, Mena shook her head at her.

"What? I am dying of thirst, and I know you are, too!"

"Kitty, let me try the water first, just in case there is something wrong with it, okay?"

"Why do you have to play the hero, Mena? We'll both try the water. That way, if it is poisonous, we both can die in this hell hole, and neither one of us is alone out here. Okay?" Mena nodded with

Kitty, and they both scooped up a handful of the water and drank it. They sat there, letting the time pass by, expecting the worst to happen.

"It tasted like water, and I feel okay. What about you, Kit?"

"I guess if it was poisonous, we would have felt something by now. Come on, drink more so that we can jump in and wash the sweat and dirt off. The water looks like heaven," Kitty said, already going for more water.

After drinking their fill, they lay back staring at their surroundings. "You know, I'd say we're handling this pretty damn well, given our circumstance. Maybe we're in shock or something. This place seems normal in so many ways, but then there are those moons in the sky and that freaky blue sand." Not getting a reply back, Mena turned her head to see Kitty by the edge of the water taking her clothing off. Watching her dive naked into the water, Mena couldn't help but smile.

Resurfacing a few feet away, Kitty yelled, "Come on, the water feels fabulous!"

Chapter Four

Mena took her clothing off as well and made her way over to the edge. Enjoying the water, Mena didn't hear the branches snapping all around them or the heavy fall of footsteps.

"All right, come on, we need to walk some more and see if we can find that portal thing again," Mena said.

Mena made her way out of the water, Kitty following behind her. Mena walked over to where her clothing was and bent to gather it. A boot stepped into her line of vision—a very, very large boot. She backed up and kept her head low, her eyes still on the boots. Slowly moving her eyes up, her every sense was on high alert. The strong smell of leather engulfed her as she took in huge thighs the size of tree trunks. A bulge that made her swallow just from the sheer size of it seemed to take up her entire line of vision. Muscles rippled under a smooth, hairless chest, the skin a golden bronze. She swallowed, not from fear, but from what... excitement? Her heart pounded quickly, heat consuming her every being. Arousal washed through her as she continued to stare at the most glorious male body she had ever seen. She should have been embarrassed by her blatant staring, but no, all she could think about was the purely male body in front of her. As she continued to stare, she noted the massive size of his forearms and biceps. The veins roped their way under his skin, standing in stark contrast. When her eyes finally reached his face, she felt her mouth drop open in amazement.

He was close to seven feet tall and nearly three hundred pounds of solid, rippling muscle! Mena craned her neck back just to look into his face. He showed no emotion, his expression making him look ruthless. His hair was short, cropped and the color of midnight. The color of his eyes boarded on eerie, an ice-blue that seemed to stare straight into her soul. A dark leather band wrapped around his forehead with strange tribal-like words written on the circumference.

Although she feared him on some level, she couldn't help the arousal that burned inside of her. He wasn't handsome in the classic sense, but the air of power and danger that surrounded him made him attractive in his own right. She brought her eyes back down and noted his chest sported tattoos in the same writing and tribal designs as the leather band around his forehead.

The tattoos began just above his nipples, working in a swirling pattern that disappeared over his shoulders. The same leather bands wrapped around both of his biceps, and tribal designs were tattooed around his forearms.

Who or what is this?

She snapped her eyes up to his face, and noted that his eyes roamed up and down her body. She suddenly remembered her nakedness, her nipples choosing that exact moment to bead into small pearls. She would have covered herself, but a mixture of fear and shock held her still. His eyes moved back to her face, startling her. Half his mouth went into a grin, one eyebrow rising as his eyes kept moving down to her breasts and back to her face.

Hearing a scream brought Mena back into reality. She stared in horror as twenty men of the same gargantuan proportions stepped out of the trees. Her eyes widened as another giant threw Kitty over his shoulder.

"Hey, you bastard, let her go!" Mena turned to run toward Kitty just as huge hands grabbed her by the waist and turned her around. Wide-eyed and frightened, Mena came face to face with the ice-blue-eyed man. The arousal she felt just moments ago vanished when she saw the smile on his lips. Fear seized her entire body, and even the act of breathing seeming difficult. She felt dizzy, uncoordinated, and all she wanted to do was make sure Kitty was okay. Her skin broke out in a light sweat, her heart beating so fast and hard she felt as if it would break through her ribs. Everything around her spun, and she felt herself start to fall. Before she hit the hard ground, big arms caught her.

* * * *

Demariak looked down at the small woman he held in his arms. A truly beautiful creature. He couldn't keep his eyes off of her and kept catching himself skimming every curve and hollow of her body. Her lips were luscious, red, and slightly swollen. Small droplets of water coated the surface, and every part of him wanted to lower his head and lick them off. She had long beautiful hair, the dark strands feeling like silk against his chest.

He watched her from the trees, the image of her glorious body swimming beneath the water causing his cock to harden painfully. Her breasts skimmed the surface of the water, the sun catching the droplets that slid off of them. He gritted his teeth at his arousal—the strongest he had ever felt before—licking through him like a flame through wood. Even though her eyes were closed, he remembered all too well how the light gray brightened as she laughed. He stared at her feet and swept her body with his eyes, taking in the smoothness of her creamy skin. Her feet were small and delicate, the toenails painted a light pink. She had long smooth legs, their smoothness making him picture them wrapped around his waist. Taking his eyes higher, he noted that she hardly had any hair covering her mound, only a small trimmed strip hiding her cleft. Her curves went on for miles, the sight making his cock stand erect and feel tight in his leathers. Her breasts were large, smooth globes big enough to fill his hands. Both were tipped with dusky rose nipples with little droplets of water still clinging to them, begging for his mouth to lick them off.

His cock grew harder at the very sight of her. He led his men through the jungle of Timanta to his kingdom high in the Bolla-Ta

Mountains. He turned around and saw his second in command, Keirak, holding the other small female. He didn't miss how Keirak's eyes strayed to the blonde woman's breasts and trimmed mound. Demariak smiled and turned back around, making his way through the thick foliage. He looked down at the female in his arms and brought her body closer to his. Whispering in her ear, he couldn't help the words that spilled forth.

"ThallaThalla te vata kenna calla ka bakatha."

My sweet, you don't know it yet, but you are already mine.

* * * *

Mena felt like she was in a dream. She tried to sift through the fog in her mind. Her eyes still closed, she could hear two deep, muffled male voices talking close by. She slowly opened her eyes, and blinked them a couple of times. The dimly lit room's candle glow left the edges in soft shadow. The ceiling was black and brightly polished. Intricate carvings covered the stone in swirling patterns. Looking around, she could hear deep male voices. More alert, she realized the voices came through a closed door.

She sat up and looked around the room. Black polished stone glistened above and below her, the same intricate swirling patterns covering every inch. She reached to her side, running her hands over the smooth marble-like stone. The carvings felt rough beneath her fingertips, every bump and indentation easily distinguishable. A white rug covered the floor, and no décor covered the walls. In each corner of the room sat a small white table. A thick pillar candle sat in the center of each table, a sweet smell coming from the burning wicks. Looking down she noticed she wasn't on a traditional bed. A stone slab acted as the bed's frame, and the mattress was filled with a fluffy substance. The sheets were red and felt like a combination of silk and velvet. The pillows had the same texture, and the same fluffy material filled their confines.

The door opened with a soft click, and a large shadow stood in the threshold.

"Malltaka ventamma boltasta."

Her heart pounding fiercely in her chest, and she swallowed roughly. She lightly shook her head. "I don't... I don't know what you're saying." She really wished her voice didn't sound so much like a whisper.

"I am sorry. I should have realized you do not speak my tongue. I go by Demariak. Do you know where you are?"

His accent was thick and heavy, his voice deep and purely male. He stepped through the door, the light seeping over his features. Her eyes widened as his features became clear, recognition making her heart start to pound wildly. Everything came rushing back to her. Swimming with Kitty... the man—the very large man... and then the darkness that overtook her.

Tilting her head back, she saw hard-set, ice-blue eyes, and a very masculine face with sharp angles.

Remembering how he looked when she first saw him seemed like a dream now that he stood so close and half naked again in front of her. He wore nothing but leather pants, the material covering his massive legs He didn't have the leather bands on, and his hair was disheveled, which seemed to soften his features slightly.

She gazed at him and couldn't help but notice his impressively sculpted chest. The tattoos he sported on his chest and forearms had the same designs as the engravings all over the room.

His height and muscular body made her feel petite for once in her life. She couldn't help the fact that her eyes traveled down to the very huge bulge that strained against his leather pants.

"Please, if you would cover yourself." When he cleared his throat, Mena didn't miss how his tone went grave and deep. His eyes flickered to her chest and back up to her face as she quickly looked down. She realized the sheet pooled at her waist, her breasts bare, her nipples stiff.

"Oh, I didn't even realize." Covering up with the sheet, she glanced at him and couldn't help but swallow as she saw the bulge in his pants get bigger. Her body became hot, and she slowly brought her eyes up to his face. He greeted her with an ice-blue gaze that reflected lust. His breathing got shallower, his body tensed, and his fists kept clenching and unclenching.

She cleared her throat and brought her eyes down. She knew she should be scared of this man, but for some odd reason she didn't feel the fear she had felt earlier when he first approached her.

He could have hurt you when you passed out, Mena, but he didn't, and he hasn't made any moves to do so now.

She looked back up at him. "My friend--her name is Kitty. Is she okay? Can I see her? Make sure she isn't scared or hurt?" Holding her breath, she waited for his reply.

"Your fair-haired companion is fine and not hurt. My second in command, Keirak, took care of all of her needs, and she will meet with you in the gathering chamber when you are feeling up to it. I have to say, she is a feisty one. Gave Keirak some trouble, but that's what he needs."

He smiled and went to a door that was hidden in the wall and pushed it open. From what she could see by craning her neck around his wide shoulders, it seemed to be a closet. He walked in easily and pulled a red box off one of the shelves, bringing it to the bed and setting it in front of her. "I will be happy to answer any questions you have. Soon it will be the last meal, and I would be most pleased if you attended. Your companion, of course, has already agreed to join us for the last meal after we assured her you would be there unharmed. So please, it would honor me greatly and put your friend's mind at ease if you would come."

Staring up at him, she clutched the sheet closely to her naked body. "Well, first off, can you please tell me where I am?" she said, trying to sound calm and confident. She didn't do as well as she hoped. Demariak slowly—as if knowing she was still unsure of him—sat on the edge of the bed, his big body almost hanging off of it.

"You speak the language of English, so I can only assume you came from a portal of sorts. Is this to be true?" Speaking slowly he stared at her, and she already knew he knew the answer.

"Yes, Kitty and I went through that portal thing and ended up here… wherever *here* is." Swallowing, she waited for his reply.

"How do I explain this?" he asked as if talking to himself. He looked at the ceiling and thought for a second. "Where you are at is called the *Dimi of the Seven Moons*. You passed through a portal, which led you here. You are still on Earth, so to speak, but have just passed into another dimension. The portal that you and your friend saw only happens once a month, and the location is unknown."

She held her breath. *The portal that you and your friend saw only happens once a month, and the location is unknown.* Luckily, she was sitting, because, at that moment, she felt herself get lightheaded.

"Wait a second." She closed her eyes, and held out a hand as if to stop him. "What do you mean once a month? I can't sit around in this place that long!" Her voice rose in panic, and she willed herself to calm down. "Anyway, if that *portal* is unknown, how do you know it only comes once a month?" She thought this might be some sick joke, and waited for his answer with a dry mouth.

"We have the ability to predict… certain things. It is the same concept as seeing something in your sky at a certain time, such as a comet, but we just can't know where it will be. It is strictly found on luck. Maybe one day that will change."

She shook her head once again and felt like Alice down the rabbit hole. Oh, what must Kitty be going through? Mena didn't think of herself as aggressive, but compared to Kitty, she was a bitch.

"This can't be real," she said, absently talking to herself. He wore the same stoic expression, his features hard and fierce.

"I am sorry you think this isn't reality, but I assure you it is. You must have noticed you are not home, yes?" He waved a hand around the room as if to emphasize his point and looked her square in the eye. He spoke to her as if she were a child. She straightened her shoulders and lifted her chin, taking offense at his tone.

"Yes, this sounds a little crazy and scary. If the roles were reversed, you know damn well you would think so, too. Yes, I realize I am not at home!" She waved her hand around the room in a mock gesture and stared back at him, "I appreciate all you have done for Kitty and me, but if it's all the same, I would like to find another way home if that damn portal won't show itself for a whole fucking month!" She knew she should probably watch her language since pissing off the giant sitting in front of her probably wasn't the wisest move. Fuck it. She let her anger take control. Feeling her ire rise at the look of amusement on his face, her body grew warm with irritation.

She watched as he moved fluidly off the bed like an animal stalking through the jungle. He walked over toward the hidden door, stopping and turning back to face her.

"I will just be outside of the door, waiting to accompany you to the gathering chamber if you choose to attend. I will remind you your friend will expect you there." He left and lightly shut the door.

Mena sat in silence, her gaze trained on the closed door, her irritation rising with each breath she took.

Chapter Five

Looking down at herself, Mena couldn't believe Demariak actually expected her to wear the black, sheer, gauzy dress. It dipped low in the front with only miniscule straps at the shoulders. The dress fell to her ankles, which would have been great if the thing wasn't transparent.

Who the hell wears something like this out in front of people?

Picking at the fabric with her hand, she agreed it was a beautiful dress. That was, if she were planning on seducing someone. He actually expected her to eat a meal in front of people with this thing on? The very thought sent a shiver down her spine. The fabric clung to her full breasts, the friction of the fabric against her skin making her nipples impossibly hard and sensitive. The dress clung to every curve and showcased her sex for all to see. Shaking her head, she went to the door and opened it, making sure that only her face and neck showed.

She saw Demariak in the corner talking with a man who looked like the total opposite of him. The stranger's hair was short, a little longer then Demariak's, giving it a shaggy, just-got-out-of-bed appearance. The color bordered on white, the blond locks so light. Under the lighting she saw streaks of gold running through it. He stood just a few inches shorter than Demariak but was still impressively built. She couldn't really see his face but knew he probably wore the same ruthlessly intense look as Demariak. Clearing her throat, she waited for Demariak to look at her.

Turning his head, he stopped talking and walked toward her. "What is it you need, *thalla*?"

"Um, well, you see, the thing you gave me to wear is, well, um… transparent. You don't actually expect me to wear this, do you?" Her face became hot with embarrassment, and she didn't miss the smirk that Demariak quickly hid.

"You are in the *ZorZack* colony now, and I know you are not accustomed to our ways, but this is what our females wear when they're not nude." She saw him hide a smile and grew frustrated. She gripped the door, shock resonating throughout her whole body.

She spoke through her teeth, not hiding the anger that showed itself. "I can't go out and eat with people wearing this thing. I don't even know you or the people that will be there. Where are the clothes I had with me?"

"We couldn't gather your clothing because the moons were to rise soon, and it can be unsafe out in the open during that time. I didn't know you would faint, so I worried more about getting you and Kitty to safety before the moons rose. I assure you that what I saw should not make you feel uncomfortable, Thalla."

"What do you mean *unsafe*?"

"There are creatures that only come out when the moons rise, creatures that are more dangerous than you can even imagine."

She stared at him, wanting to know more but hesitant to ask. In the end, though, her curiosity got the better of her. "What kind of creatures?"

He watched her, his body half shrouded in the shadows. "Creatures that tear you to pieces with knife-like teeth. There are creatures that only drink blood and then leave the bodies to rot on the ground. Predators that only have to touch you for their poison to get into your body. Believe me when I say you don't want to be out there when the moons are high."

She could only stare at him in shock. The creatures he described where something out of a nightmare. She couldn't believe creatures like the ones he described really existed, and just beyond the enclosure she was in. "Really?" She knew how stupid the comment sounded, but it automatically came out. She didn't know how else to respond.

He nodded, his face serious as he watched her. She shook her head, wanting to get the sudden, horrible images of those creatures out of her mind.

"It would be a great disrespect for you not to follow our customs while you are here."

She was thankful for the change of subject. "Okay, well, I don't know if I want to know all about what happens when the moons come up since Kitty and I slept outside last night, but maybe later you can explain a little more to me." She said it more as a statement than a question.

"Anything that you may wish to know you have only to ask." Trapping her gaze, his gravely, deep voice did something to make her nipples tingle and her pussy start to weep.

Oh, how crazy am I? Get yourself together, Mena. Now is not the time or place to be getting all hot and bothered. Something must have happened to me when I went through that damned portal.

She closed her eyes and shook her head. She knew nothing changed her when she went through the portal. She would have to be blind not to know that this man oozed sex appeal, making the very junction between her legs become wet with wanting to be filled.

Looking back up at him, Mena didn't want to seem disrespectful to the man who claimed he brought Kitty and her to safety.

For now it might do me well to play nice until Kitty and I can find another way home. This man and his people may be friends, but until I know for sure, I better play it safe.

She threw her inhibitions aside and opened the door to reveal herself to Demariak.

Mena walked down a long hallway, Demariak in front of her, his body tense. After basically flashing herself to him, she got a little self conscious when he hadn't said anything. She looked down at herself once more, running her hands over the smooth material.

Come on, Mena, what are you hoping for? Do you really want him to throw you over his shoulder and do deliciously wicked things to you?

Getting vivid pictures of that act in her head, she clenched her legs together as best she could. She could feel her clit throb with the beat of her heart and her juices start to coat her pussy lips. Veering off to the left, they entered a large room with white stone floors and white polished stone walls.

He led her through a small, quiet hallway. She wasn't even hungry, but she agreed to all of this because he told her Kitty would be there. She couldn't even imagine how Kitty was holding up. She picked at the dress, a *stonna* he called it.

The dress looked even more ridiculous on her than she could have imagined. She admitted, though, it did showcase her assets perfectly. He told her all the females wore this when not nude, and that gave her a little bit of courage. She at least wouldn't be too noticeable in it… she hoped.

"Are we close?"

She felt like they walked for miles, every turn looking like the last. He turned back, his eyes roaming over her body as he smiled and nodded. She shivered, arousal coursing through her body again. How could one look from him cause her to become so sensitive? So aroused?

* * * *

Walking into a large dining room, surprise filled Mena at what she saw. The room itself was fairly large, many of the seats around the table enormous. The stone walls and flooring had the same patterns carved into them as every other wall. The colors seemed to vary in each room, this one combining red and black.

The only lighting that illuminated the room came from candles scattered sporadically. An enormous chandelier made up of some type of cloudy glass hung in the center the room. The banquet-sized table sat in the center of the room, bare except for dishes and goblets. The top of it had a giant circle carved into it with the familiar writing and tribal designs inside the circle. Several thick stone chairs sat on either side of the table, many of them filled with fearsome looking men. Many of the men sported bare chests, showcasing their perfect physiques. Three chairs at the head of the table sat empty.

Demariak lightly placed his hand on the small of Mena's back and led her to the foot of the table. As soon as they reached the end of the table, all of the men stood at once, turned toward them, and bowed their heads. Getting nervous about her nearly nude appearance among so many large and virile men, she quickly flung one arm across her breasts and the other hand to cover her mound.

Feeling the warmth of Demariak's hand on her back, Mena felt her arousal start to grow again. His hand nearly covered her whole lower back. She didn't know what to expect. She looked back and forth between the men and Demariak. They all wore leather pants ranging in color from creamy white to pitch black.

"Mena, these are my warriors."

"Your warriors?" She knew Demariak held himself in an air of authority, but he called them *his* warriors, and that implied he lead them. It wasn't hard to believe since Demariak's presence screamed command and leadership.

"Yes, these are some of my warriors from the first line. The rest of them have been sent to a neighboring village and aren't expected back for some time. I am the leader of the *ZorZack* tribe, as was my father, grandfather, and so on and so forth."

Swallowing roughly, Mena nodded and stared at the men Demariak introduced. Going down the line, he first introduced a large, fearsome-looking man with black hair shaved close to his skull. His eyes were intense and dark, the midnight orbs showing no emotion. Demariak called him Draydon. Mena shook herself at the chill that went down her spine, the dead look he gave her making goose bumps rise over her flesh. All the men had a certain air about them, a power that made one fear them. Something seemed off about Draydon. He expelled a stronger aura of danger and menace that coated every part of him.

The next man's hair brushed his shoulders. He tied it at the nape of his neck, the sandy colored strands pulling away from his square features. He called him Icezak. She instantly felt the uneasiness that she got from Draydon wash away. Icezak's eyes were the color of sapphires, and she felt a calmness with him. She pictured him as the gentle one of the bunch. A friendly smile played across his lips. She didn't doubt how powerful he was, but something about him put her at ease.

Turning to the other side of the table he introduced her to "the twins". He called them Merak and Adriak, both almost identical in appearance except for their unique hair. Both their hair fell to their shoulders, but Merak's was a deep bronze with blond highlights, and Adriak's a sandy blond with bronze highlights. Both had eyes the color of burnt amber.

"Shortly Keirak will be escorting Kitty to the gathering chamber." Hearing the deep rumble of Demariak's voice, Mena turned her head his way. Hearing what he said, but not quite registering it, she kept thinking about how not a single one of the men had said one word to her.

She looked at Demariak to question him about it when she heard Kitty's familiar voice yelling down the hall. Turning toward the open doorway, Mena hid a smile at what she saw. Kitty was being dragged by the enormous man Mena had seen Demariak speaking with earlier, whom she took to be Keirak. Now that he wasn't turned at an angle, Mena's eyes widened when she noted that his eye color rivaled that of a fresh lime. The closer he got, she noted a black ring circled the outside of the iris.

"Get your fucking meaty hands off me, you barbarian! I told you I would go wherever you took me without a fight if Mena would be there." Mena smiled as she saw Kitty wearing the same gauzy-looking dress as she wore. Kitty twisted out of his grip and turned around with her hands on her hips. Never having seen this side of her before, Mena watched Kitty with her mouth going slightly slack.

I guess in any circumstance anyone can snap.

"Don't you have anything to say? You have been by my side the whole day and haven't said one damn word to me!"

The man stared at Kitty while his fists clenched and his jaw worked. He turned toward Demariak, his eyes doing a slow sweep of Kitty's barely-hidden body. In a deep, low voice, he spoke directly to Demariak. "Thannoja vankclack benna ta, balletka te manolla."

Mena saw Demariak smile, her curiosity piquing as to what had been said.

"Kitty!" Rushing over to her, she threw her arms around Kitty, crushing her in a bear hug.

"Are you okay? That barbarian over there wouldn't speak to me when I would ask about you." Tilting her head toward Keirak, Kitty didn't even look over to acknowledge him. "Look at this thing he brought me to wear! I look like I should be on the freaking street corner waiting to get fucked! I yelled at him to bring me my clothes, but he just looked at me and shoved the damn thing toward me more. I put it on thinking this was the only way they would let me see you. Anyway, I'm certainly not walking around this place naked, so I guess this will have to do."

Looking down at herself, Mena felt the beginning of actual amusement at their predicament. "Well, at least we can look like sluts together," she said, with a smile in her voice. After making sure they were both unharmed, they went to their seats. Demariak gestured for Mena to sit next to him at the head of the table and for Kitty to sit next to her. Keirak then sat at the end, diagonal to Kitty, which made Kitty look at him, turning back with a scowl on her face. After they sat down, all of the men talked freely among themselves in their language. Feeling intrigued watching them speak with themselves, Mena didn't notice the women who stepped through the doorway, carrying huge trays.

Chapter Six

"What...the...?" Looking in front of her, Mena's eyes widened. Her mouth going slack, she watched as ten *naked* women walked into the room with platters and trays overflowing with strange food. Even though Demariak had told her the females of his tribe went naked most of the time, shock still went through her at the sight. The women made their way around the room with their small or large-sized breasts bouncing along. As her eyes drifted south, she noted that all of the women were completely shaved. The women came in all shapes and sizes, all equally beautiful in their own exotic way. Their hair must have been long because every one of them swept it up in tasteful knots on their heads with pieces coming down and framing their faces.

A petite but large-breasted redhead came up to the man called Icezak. With her head down, she spoke softly to him in their language. Mena watched as Icezak caressed one of her breasts, nodding and speaking softly to her. The redhead's breathing picked up, and her eyes slowly drifted closed. Icezak took hold of both of her breasts, gave a good squeeze, and brought her to sit facing him on his leather-clad lap, which, of course, made her legs spread apart.

She felt weird for watching, but, unable to take her eyes off the scene in front of her, she stared as Icezak kept a constant squeeze on both breasts. He then licked a path up her neck toward her mouth where he took possession of it with extreme force.

Clearly the woman was enjoying herself if the little moans and gasps were anything to go by. Mena looked over at Kitty and saw that she, too, watched the scene but with little interest.

"Lord, Kitty, you don't look the least bit surprised about this," Mena said in a hushed tone as she stared at Kitty.

Facing Mena, Kitty shrugged her shoulders and started picking out food from the many platters. "Those naked chicks have been walking all day. I guess I'm used to it." Shrugging her shoulders again, she nibbled on the food in front of her. Mena could not believe the turnaround Kitty seemed to make since they had fallen down the "rabbit hole".

What happened to the soft spoken, shy Kit I know?

She turned back to the scene that became more explicit by the second.

Having moved from the woman's mouth, Icezak brought his mouth to her breasts and popped a stiff nipple into his mouth, sucking it, making it get impossibly longer. He slid one of his hands between the woman's legs. Mena craned her neck just to get a peek. Feeling herself blush, she looked around to make sure no one saw her acting like a voyeur. After several moments of his fingers delving, no doubt, in the woman's pussy, she got on her knees and slipped under the table. Sitting up straighter, Mena tried not to let her curiosity about what was going on under there get the best of her.

* * * *

Demariak watched as Mena saw the naked females bring in the trays of food and didn't miss how her eyes widened as they went around the room. Looking over at her, he didn't miss the curiosity in her face at what Kenna did to Icezak under the table. If she only knew what happened when the meal actually finished. Inhaling slowly, he looked over at Mena again and did a slow sweep of her gauze-covered body.

Her nipples stood erect, and it surprised him that they hadn't cut through the fabric. Her breathing had gone shallower, her tongue running over her lips. He could smell her arousal, the sweet honey that flowed out of her plump pussy lips. What he wouldn't give to throw her on his bed, spread her legs, and suck on her juicy pussy. He would then take her swollen clit between his lips and suck it until she screamed his name, her honey sliding down his throat. He cleared his throat and glanced at her with heavy-lidded eyes, his cock giving a mighty jerk through his pants.

Oh, my sweet, soon you'll be mine.

* * * *

Not wanting to seem too obvious, but having her curiosity nag at her, Mena slowly pulled up the bottom of the tablecloth and watched in awe at the display before her. Her eyes slowly widened as she saw the redheaded woman on her knees with her hands placed on Icezak's big, muscular thighs.

The redhead pulled his pants down and threw them out of the way. She encased his huge cock in her mouth and worked it like it was dinner and she hadn't eaten anything in forever. She watched as the redhead slowly pulled the cock out of her mouth to take hold of his balls and gently knead them. She ever so slowly stuck her tongue out and licked the spit-glistened head and then took the whole length into her mouth again, bobbing up and down while gripping the base of his cock with her hand.

Feeling her face get hot and her labia become moist, Mena straightened back up in her seat and was surprised to see Demariak staring at her. His hands tightly held on to the edge of the table, and he slowly inhaled. Leaning close to her ear, he whispered to her as he brought his hand down on her knee, "Do you realize, *thalla*, that I can smell the sweet moisture that is pooling between your legs right now?"

Gasping, she pulled away, and looked him in the eyes.

"Does it turn you on to watch Kenna sucking Icezak's cock? Do you wish you were the one on your knees taking it in your mouth?"

As he slowly rubbed his hand up and down her thigh, Mena clenched her legs together to stop the wetness from slipping out and running down her leg. Sure, the act she just saw turned her on, but what really got her worked up was the deep, almost growl of Demariak's voice and the sexual things he said in her ear. Pulling her leg away from his hand, she cleared her throat.

"I don't know what you mean about *smelling* me, but I assure you that type of behavior does not… make me excited."

Not even commenting back to her, he gave her that oh-so-sexy half smirk and righted himself in the chair. She watched as a curvy brunette with apple-sized breasts and pierced nipples set a large platter of strange fruit next to her. The items on the tray were different but appeared similar to the fruit she knew back home. She reached over to the tray and grabbed what looked like bright blue raspberries. She brought them to her nose and inhaled deeply before popping a few in her mouth. She closed her eyes, moaned inaudibly, and savored the taste that exploded in her mouth. The fruit tasted like a combination of strawberry and blueberry, a sweet concoction that tantalized her taste buds. Grabbing another handful of the berries, she popped them in her mouth and looked over at Kitty to see her friend staring at Keirak. She noticed Kitty doing that a lot tonight, whether she realized it or not. She offered some berries to Kitty, trying to get her attention off of Keirak. Kitty waved her hand away, not even looking at Mena as she moved the food around on her plate. She would have offered Kitty some encouragement or sympathy or something to cheer her up, but what should she say? They were both stuck here, and until they could find a way out, they might as well try to deal with it.

She reached over to grab some more berries when a large, roughened hand landed on her arm. Scrunching her face together, she turned toward Demariak, eyed his big hand on her arm, and then looked him dead in the eye.

"What the hell do you think you're doing? I am starving!" She lifted up her chin a notch, her hunger making her courageous. He leaned in close to her again, his warm breath tickling her neck right below her ear. Shivering at the desire that swamped her from the simple act, she turned her head slightly so they were almost nose to nose.

"*Thalla*, as much as I would like for you to eat a whole platter of the *deyada* berries, I feel it would be cruel of me not to warn you first." His deep voice shot straight to where she wanted him the most, making her clit tingle with awareness. Confusion assaulted her at his comment.

"What do you mean, warn me? Am I not supposed to eat those? Will I get sick?" Looking at the berries, she turned toward Kitty. Before she could warn her, Demariak's warm palm landed on her upper thigh, stopping her.

"I don't mean to frighten you, *thalla*. The berries will not harm you. It's just that those particular berries are saved for after the last meal because of their… side effects." He slowly rubbed circles on her thigh, as he spoke the words softly.

* * * *

Demariak watched as Mena ate berry after berry. His cock grew had as her ripe red lips sucked them in, her tongue licking the juice off of her mouth. He knew the *deyada* berries would kick in shortly, leaving Mena desperately wanting sexual gratification. The berries were used as the *dessert* when the warriors' hunger had been sated, but when another kind of *hunger* presented itself. How would Mena react to the knowledge that after the last meal of the evening the gathering chamber broke out into a large orgy of sweat-soaked bodies rubbing on each other?

As he tried to explain more, she stopped him. He didn't want her to be unaware, but if she refused to hear what he had to say then he would sit back and enjoy the show. The *deyada* berries would take effect very soon. He leaned back in his seat, a smile covering his lips as he watched Mena eat more of the berries. What she didn't know was that the *deyada* berries were a natural aphrodisiac, one so potent it wouldn't take very long for them to kick in.

Chapter Seven

She finished up the meal, sat back and watched everyone around her. Her belly grew warm and tingly, and she idly rubbed it as she sat up straighter. Clearing her throat, she grabbed something to drink to see if that might cool her down. Inside of her a fire lit, her very fingertips tingling with warmth.

She looked over at Demariak, a smile covering his lips. She scowled at him, not thinking any of this was funny. She looked down at the food, wondering what was in it. Maybe she should have listened to Demariak? She clenched her teeth, her nipples puckering up and rubbing against the fabric of her dress. She rubbed her legs together, trying desperately to ease the ache between her legs. Every move of her legs caused her pussy lips to slide together, pinching her clit between them.

"How do you feel, *thalla*?" Demariak threw his big muscled arm over the back of her chair, making it seem like he loomed over her. Clearing her throat, she did her best not to make it obvious that his voice did something sexual to her.

"Actually, I think I'm ready to go to bed now. I'm pretty tired." She breathed in deeply and tried to look like she actually meant what she just said.

Yeah right, tired my ass! I need to touch myself before I explode.

She did a quick sweep up Demariak's body, suppressing a shiver of delight at the obvious erection pressing against his pants. The heat in her belly grew and moved throughout her body, making her nipples grow sensitive. Her core swelled with need, and the juices from her pussy lips trickled down her leg.

She needed to be alone fast and felt like a fool for the insane feelings going on inside of her. She didn't know what else to do, so she turned toward Kitty, and quickly told her that she would be back later.

She rushed down the hall, all but running to her room. She momentarily stopped to catch her breath, braced herself against the smooth wall and clenched her thighs together. The sweet pressure only seemed to inflame her desire, making her softly moan to herself. A hand brushed against the nape of her neck. Her head rose as she tightened her jaw at how exquisite the simple touch felt.

"Are you okay, *thalla*? You ran out of there so quickly, I thought you might have been ill." His voice was rough against her ear. He slowly pressed his leather-covered erection lightly against her back, eliciting a moan from her. She suppressed a shiver of delight when he gently thrust against her. His erection was huge against her back, every curve and vein prominent even through the material.

She knew she shouldn't be engaging Demariak in anything sexual, but her need was so intense it was hard to push him away.

Oh my, you're acting like a crazed schoolgirl right now! You just met him. You're in a strange world, and all you can think about is having sex?

A part of her brain knew that what was happening shouldn't, but the other side of her brain screamed for sexual release.

The material covering her breasts felt far too rough and made her stiff nipples tingle. She could feel her vagina swell impossibly more, and the juices now ran freely down her thighs, making her lips rub deliciously together.

His hot breath tickled the nape of her neck, and she laid her head back on his massive, hard chest and felt his large hand move to cover her belly.

"Oh, *thalla*, what you do to me." He growled as he dragged his hand up her belly and over her rib cage to cup one breast in his hand. Bringing his other hand in front as well, he brought it up to the other breast and tweaked both of her hard nipples. She moaned from his touch.

"It was those damn berries, wasn't it? Why didn't you tell me not to eat them?" The statement came out on a moan. She closed her eyes at the pure pleasure his wicked fingers caused.

"*Thalla*, I tried to tell you, but you didn't want to hear anymore." Demariak slowly licked from the curve of her neck to her ear, where he swirled his tongue around and then gently bit down. She gasped and brought her hands up to cover his. She urged him to squeeze harder, and breathed in deeply as he continued to take both of her nipples between his thumbs and forefingers and tweak them.

She gasped in delight as he scooped her up in his arms and quickly carried her to his chamber, slamming the door behind him with his foot. She was about to say something but gasped as he pressed her back against the door. Before anything could be said, Demariak took possession of her mouth. His firm and warm lips moved against hers, his motions that of a starved man. She could feel the hot, hard length of him pressed into her belly, making her moan into his mouth. Demariak swirled his tongue around hers, sucking hers back into his mouth with a possessiveness Mena had never known. He broke the kiss and rested his forehead on hers and breathed heavily.

* * * *

Kitty watched as Mena rushed out of the room and barely missed the naked women in the process. Demariak followed her out, his movements slow and predatory. It reminded Kitty of a wild animal stalking its prey. She stood and made her move to follow Mena, not wanting her to be alone with that barbarian. She slipped between the women, barely missing their naked flesh, and stepped into the hall. It was a catacomb of tunnels, turns, and dips that made it impossible to find out which way they went. She took a blind leap of faith and veered off to the left, knowing Mena hadn't gotten that far.

She walked for ten minutes before she stopped and leaned against the wall. She was lost. Every wall, every turn looked exactly the same as the one before. She wanted to scream out in frustration. She slid to the ground, pulling her knees to her shoulders and staring at the smooth ceiling. As worried as she was about Mena, she knew Mena could take care of herself. Mena was a strong, fierce woman in her own right, a female that could hold her own. She at least hoped her instincts were right because God help anyone who hurt her. "What am I going to do?" Her head fell back against the smooth, cold surface, and she closed her eyes, not knowing where to go from here.

Loud footsteps neared, and she slowly opened her eyes. She wasn't surprised to see Keirak standing in front of her, his posture stiff, his expression stern. She didn't know why he insisted on following her around, only giving her privacy in the room he stuck her in. She didn't bother saying anything, knowing he couldn't understand a thing she said. Walking past him, she went back toward the dining room, not knowing where else to go. She wanted to go to her room, to just sleep and wake up and have this all be a bad dream. When she reached the dining room, she stood at the entrance, not going in, just standing there. Her eyes stayed on Keirak, telling him without saying a word where she wanted to go. He was smarter than he looked, not just brawn and no brain. She followed him, knowing there would have been no way she would have found her own way back. Because of the twisting turns, everything looked exactly the same.

He opened the door for her and stepped out of the way, giving her plenty of room. She slowly went into the room, her eyes constantly on him. "Do you know where Mena is?"

His brows dipped over his eyes, the confusion clear on his face.

"Oh never mind." She shut the door quickly, wanting to be alone, wanting to shut out everything around her.

* * * *

"Oh, *thalla*, I should stop."

Feeling Demariak's large hands flex and release on her hips, Mena knew she should tell him to stop, but the fire running through her body could not be ignored.

"No, Demariak, don't stop… I need you to put out the burning inside of me."

She stared at him, and saw his nostrils flare and his eyes glaze over with lust. Ready this time, Mena took his kiss and gave back just as forcefully. She nibbled on his mouth and took satisfaction at the groan that escaped his lips. She ran her tongue over his lips and thrusted her tongue inside his mouth. Demariak let out a pure male growl of satisfaction, but soon took over the kiss, showing his dominance.

He ran his hand up her rib cage, skimming the sides of her breasts to grip the edge of her dress. He ripped the fabric down to her navel, immediately taking possession of one of her breasts with his mouth. He swirled his tongue around the already stiff peak, drawing it between his teeth, giving it a little tug.

She moaned and threw her head back, grabbing Demariak's wide shoulders for support. His hot breath skimmed over her breasts, causing her to suck in a deep breath of air. He moved from her nipple and licked a path between her breasts and up the column of her neck, lightly sucking and scraping his teeth over the skin below her ear. He whispered to her in his language, his words roughened by his lust. She gasped as he picked her up, carrying her to the bed and setting her lightly atop it. In one swift move, he tore the rest of her dress from her body.

"You are so beautiful."

She shivered at the harsh deepness of his voice and looked at him from under her lashes. She suddenly felt nervous and saw his hands go to his pants and unlace them. He quickly shoved them down his legs and kicked them to the side. Mena swallowed at the sight. His body was thickly muscled, all bulging muscles and sinew. She took in the wide expanse of his shoulders, the tattoos that seemed to amplify the air of power and dominance he emitted. She slowly gazed at the length of his rippled abdomen, hot wetness flowing from her at the sight of him. Every inch of him was smooth, golden skin. Her eyes drifted farther south, leading to what she wanted most at the moment.

He watched her with heavy-lidded eyes. The way his eyes traveled down her body made her vagina clench with need.

Mena held back the gasp that traveled up her throat when she caught sight of the massive erection he revealed. Demariak's erection was thick and long, being at least the width of her wrist and jutting from smooth, hairless skin. The head shone a violent red, a pearl-sized drop of liquid dotting the tip.

"Th-that won't fit." She felt stupid for even saying anything. She saw Demariak smile slowly and stalk toward her. She moved back farther on the bed, her back hitting the ice-cold wall. She knew an erection that size couldn't fit in her. The arousal in her made her think of how deliciously he would stretch and fill her. Blushing, she felt her hot juices slide down the inside of her leg from her illicit thoughts.

Her eyes grew wide as he moved onto the bed. His big body covered her, all light blocked by his sheer size. His hand covered her hip, running up to her breast and causing her flesh to prickle with awareness. He removed his hand and sat back on his haunches. A gasp came out of her when both of his warm hands landed on her thighs, gently spreading them. She held on to the sheets as his head dipped. She felt him run his tongue up and down her inner thigh, moving more toward her center. Her mouth opened on a silent cry as his tongue touched her clit, sucking it into the warm cavern of his mouth. He moaned deeply, looking up from her thighs and making eye contact with her. Mena didn't bother hiding her shock when he licked all her glistening wetness off of his lips.

Looking down at Mena's soaked pussy, Demariak spread her thighs wider, watching as she lay completely back and closed her eyes. His cock jerked at the sight of her bare, pink pussy lips, swollen and wet from her arousal. Her clit pulsed with need, ruby red from his ministrations. Sticking his tongue out, he twirled it around her clit again, sucking the little berry into his mouth. She moaned in satisfaction as he ran his tongue down her slit, plunging it into her waiting hole. Looking up, he saw her hands grabbing forcefully onto the material of the bed.

He looked at Mena with lust-filled eyes and suppressed the desire that consumed him. Her muscles tightened around his fingers, gripping him like an iron fist. He sucked harder on her clit, needing to bring her climax to the surface. She threw her head back as he sucked harder and faster. Her moan went long and loud, driving his arousal higher. He thrust his fingers faster as he felt her warm juices start to coat his hand.

* * * *

Mena sucked in her bottom lip, a moan spilling from her mouth. Demariak did wicked things to her, making her juices flow out and down her ass. He moved from her clit, plunging his tongue in and out of her hole, bringing his thumb to her clit and moving it around in slow circles. His tongue left the hot depth of her and moved along her lips, lightly nibbling them as he went. Mena gripped the sheets tighter as he sucked in her throbbing, swollen clit vigorously. He slipped two large, rough fingers into her soaked vagina, thrusting them deep. Mena felt all the pleasure build inside of her. Her inner muscles tightened, drawing Demariak's fingers in deeper.

Chapter Eight

Her body felt drained from the intense orgasm Demariak gave her. Demariak moved up her body, lying between her thighs. His hard, hot length slid sensuously up and down her center. He brought his hand up, glistening with her juices, and sucked his fingers into his mouth. Her eyes widened, and she shivered with arousal. Watching him made her dimming arousal start to burn again.

"Mmm, *thalla*, you taste of sweetness."

He licked every drop from his hand. She could feel his hard length pressing against her sex. Her pussy clenched, needing to be filled with his hard cock. A fresh coat of wetness escaped her and ran out of her. She grabbed his huge penis and couldn't help but rub her pussy along his length.

"No, *thalla*, I am on the edge, and you are tempting the beast within." His ran his hands along her flesh, clenching and unclenching his fists against her. He breathed in deeply, groaning against her mouth and running his tongue along the seam of her lips.

"I want you to be sure about this, Mena, because when I plunge deep within you, I won't be able to stop. So I will ask you only this once if you are sure."

She smiled up at him, and placed her arms above her head. "I am so ready, Demariak."

She arched her back, causing her breasts to rub against his smooth chest. Her nipples scraped erotically against the smoothness of his skin, causing them both to moan in delight. She rubbed her pussy along his length, whispering *yes*, as the head of his cock teased her clit. His look spoke of hunger and lust, a combination that excited her.

"Please, Demariak, I have never been this hot before, and I am so wet for you. If you don't fuck me now, I'll go crazy." She never felt this wild or wanton before, never spoke this erotically. She also never felt an arousal as strong as the one making her weep at just the thought of Demariak's larger-than-life cock.

She watched as he gripped his erection, which dripped large amounts of pre-cum. He placed it at the entrance of her pussy and started to push inside.

"Please, Demariak, I need all of it now!" Arching her back and moaning, she felt him growl deeply and plunge every hot, hard inch of him into her. He let out a sound of pure male satisfaction. He dipped his head, taking control of her mouth and plunging his tongue deep within. Dueling with her tongue, he pumped long and hard inside of her. The sound of wet sex echoed throughout the room.

He plunged in and out of her, her muscles rippling along his shaft. He took both of her wrists and brought them above her head, pinning them under one of his hands. He brought the other one between their bodies and stroked her clit. Her muscles flexed around him violently. She moved her head from side to side and let out a long female moan. He slammed into her once… twice, and let out a roar as his release washed into her.

Mena's orgasm seemed to go on and on. When she felt it start to subside, a long shot of hot cum would wash her insides, a new orgasm cresting inside of her. She felt the last hard pulse of Demariak's release inside of her. Her own release slowly drifted her into relaxation, making everything fuzzy around the edges. Demariak slumped over her and gave her a slow kiss, running his tongue along her teeth and nipping her bottom lip. He released her wrists and lay next to her. She felt a sense of emptiness consume her at the loss of Demariak's warm heaviness. He grabbed her by the waist and pulled her ass flush with his still rock-hard erection. He lightly kissed the nape of her neck, and she closed her eyes, a sigh of contentment coming out of her. She snuggled in closer, her ass rubbing against his cock. He growled in her ear, his teeth gently biting down. "No, *thalla*, we will wait. You must be sore, and when I take you again, I want you to be rested." His breathing grew even and deep, and she snuggled deeper into his embrace. "Demariak?"

"Yes, *thalla*."

"What does that mean? You keep calling me that, and I was just wondering." He didn't speak as he stroked her hip.

"It means *my sweet*."

Feeling a smile spread across her face, she couldn't help the happiness that a simple endearment like that would cause.

"Sleep now, *thalla*, since I can guarantee you will need all of your strength when you wake."

He pulled the soft, silky sheets over them, causing her to drift off into a peaceful slumber. She felt warm and secure wrapped in Demariak's protective embrace.

* * * *

She moaned lightly, her eyes slowly opening. Pleasure washed over her, making every cell in her body light up. Looking over her shoulder, she saw Demariak's hands caressing her ass. His mouth trailed kisses down her body, causing her skin to prickle.

"Ah, you're awake, *thalla*." He looked at her with heavy-lidded eyes. He pressed his rock-hard erection against her backside, rolling his hips and letting her soft skin caress him. He rolled her over, lifting her arms above her head and causing her breasts to thrust out. His hand slipped between their bodies, her pussy already soaking wet. His thumb found her clit and smoothed her juices across it.

She watched the erotic sight of him spreading her thighs wide and inserting two large fingers into her. She let her thighs fall open as wide as they could, letting the sweet feeling of being filled consume her. His fingers delved faster inside of her, his thumb working her clit in smooth circles. She placed her hand over his, applying just the right amount of pressure to her throbbing clit.

Pleasure built in her belly, making its way to the very tips of her fingers.

"Oh, yes. Don't stop." She breathed heavily as he removed the hand that played with her clit. About to object, she felt his hot breath and wet tongue bathe her clit with knowledgeable strokes and caresses.

Her orgasm washed through her, and she moaned out his name. After the final pulses left her body, she lay there in a sexually satisfied daze. He lay beside her, pulling her close to his body.

His hard sex pressed against her thigh, and she felt selfish for taking and not giving. She wanted to taste his hot cock in her mouth, wanted to roll her tongue around the head and taste his cum. Feeling brazen, she straddled him, rubbing her hot, wet core over his hard length. He moaned loudly, the sound enough to send her over the edge by itself. She felt his cock pulse beneath her. Sliding sensuously down his body, she let her hands feel the hard muscle beneath soft skin. His muscles flexed under her hands, the skin tightening and the veins bulging. She ran her hands down his inner thighs, the muscles clenching in response. She lowered her mouth to his cock, the tip already glistening with need.

She did a sexy slide down his body, making sure to rub every part of exposed skin. She smiled at him before her mouth encased the head of his cock. Her tongue slid over the slit of his cock, her moan vibrating against his shaft. She encased his length, her head bobbing up and down. Her hand gripped his balls, kneading them in rhythm while she sucked his cock.

She let go of his cock with a resounding pop. Her tongue ran in a long sweep across the underside of his cock, her hand never leaving his aching balls. She dipped her head low, taking his balls into the hot cavern of her mouth. He growled low in his throat, her mouth sucking him in deep, her tongue sweeping across the skin.

The sound of him gritting his teeth echoed throughout the room.

She took as much of him as she could. She could only get half of him into her mouth. She savored his musky male taste. She picked up a smooth rhythm, grabbing the base of his cock with her hand while her mouth worked him. She brought her other hand between his thighs, and gripped the huge, heavy sack that lay nestled beneath, rolling his balls in her hand. His whole body tensed, and she tasted a fresh squirt of pre-cum bathe her tongue. Bracing herself for his release, she moaned with the knowledge of what was about to come.

"*Thalla*, you must stop. I can't hold off much longer." He pleaded with her in a gravelly, sexually-laced voice. She resisted his attempts to push her away and sped up her bobbing motion. She tightened her lips around his cock, sucking him in deeper. He let out a load male groan, the hot jets of his seed hitting the back of her throat. Keeping up her motions, she swallowed every last bit of his cum. He tasted of strong virile man, and she couldn't get enough of it. He relaxed against the bed as she gave his member one last long lick. She crawled up the length of him, feeling satisfied at his release.

Chapter Nine

He ran his hands up and down her back, his still-aching erection pressed against her moist center. He flipped her over, coming to rest against her back. He grabbed her by the waist, lifting her hips up and bringing her ass flush with his groin. She braced herself on her hands and knees and pressed her ass closer into him. He ran his hand up her spine, moving her hair over and gripping her shoulder. Her back was smooth and flawless, her ass succulent and perfectly round.

He squeezed her ass, gripping the skin and parting it slightly. He was perfectly still behind her, his attention focused on the tight rosebud of her asshole. He let go of her shoulder, his hand moving to her breasts where he encased her flesh. She moaned and dropped her head between her shoulders. His hand gripped her breasts, her nipples beading from the friction. His fingers gripped her stiff nipple, tweaking it between his thumb and forefinger. His other hand squeezed her ass before smacking the cheek. She gasped, the sound making his cock jerk in response. His finger glided slowly between her cheeks and rested on the tight hole in the center.

"*Thalla*, will you let me here?" He pressed slowly against her anus, and she hesitated for a second before nodding. "Good, *thalla*, that's real good."

Bending down, he kissed both globes of her ass and pulled back to spread her cheeks wide. He squeezed both cheeks in his hands and looked at the sight before him. The rosebud between her cheeks was small and tight. He knew it would strangle his cock with pleasure when he slid it in. Her pussy lips were smooth and swollen and the most beautiful red color. Her sweet wetness dripped onto the sheets as her body prepared herself for his invasion.

He slid his fingers across her soaking center and brought the fluid to the tip of her clit, lightly stroking it. Feeling a jolt of pleasure wash over him at her sexual moan, he continued his ministrations. He brought his fingers back to her soaking pussy hole, coating them in her juices as he plunged his fingers into her. Immediately her inner muscles gripped his fingers. Her wetness dripped down his hand as she climaxed. Before her orgasm faded, he brought his soaked fingers to her asshole and coated the small hole. It glistened in the soft light, making his cock jerk hard. She tensed. He stroked her back and whispered encouragements to her in his language. Ever so slowly, he slid one finger into her and let her muscles adjust to the size.

* * * *

Mena tensed. She didn't know what to expect, since she had never let a man enter her there before. Yet she knew Demariak would never harm her. She felt his finger slip into her. Her muscles tensed at the strange and new invasion. Once she felt his whole finger in her, she felt a second one slowly slide in. She tried to relax her muscles back there, as his fingers slid completely in. With both fingers buried deep within her, he slowly spread them in a scissoring motion. A shot of pure pleasure traveled from where his fingers were, straight to her clit. Her pussy grew wet with need, her body aching to be filled in both places. Moaning loudly, she knew she should be embarrassed by her wanton behavior, but she couldn't help how her body reacted to Demariak's touch.

"That's it, *thalla*. Do you feel me filling you? I will have my cock in here next. Tell me you want me here." He turned his fingers in a slow circle, eliciting a moan from her.

"Oh… yes, Demariak, there, I want you there, in me …now." Breathing deeply, she thrust lightly back toward his fingers. She stopped as his fingers slowly pulled out. She turned, trying to see why he stopped. The bed slightly dipped as he moved off of it. He walked over to one of the small tables and pulled a silver jar out. He was behind her again in an instant, his hand smoothing over the top of her ass. Before she could ask what he had, something thin and cool slid into her. A shot of warm fluid entered her. Before she could say anything, she felt the scorching hot crown of him poised at her back entrance.

"It's lubricant, *thalla*. It is from the *pandie* flower. It will help to relax your muscles so you can take me easier."

She nodded and couldn't speak. He poised the head of his cock at her back entrance again. He pushed into her, the lubricant making it easy for him to slide inside. When the head sat inside of her, he stopped and let her adjust to the invasion. His large size felt a bit unusual, but the initial uncomfortable feeling immediately washed away when he slid completely in. Wave after wave of pleasure shot straight to her core, making her inner muscles clench around his shaft. Gripping the sheets, she let the pleasure continue to course through her body. He slowly pulled out, the head almost popping free before he plunged back inside. She looked over her shoulder, and she saw sweat trickle down his forehead. His face looked intense. He swallowed roughly and closed his eyes. He moaned in a pure male way as he slid another thick, hard inch of himself in. Turning back around, she dropped her head between her shoulders and braced her legs farther apart. She wanted to take in more of him. Breathing hard, she felt sweat trickle down into the valley of her breasts.

"Please Demariak! All of it—I need it all now."

A loud, purely animalistic growl came from him as he slammed repeatedly into her. His balls were huge, slapping repeatedly against her clit. Her entire body lit up with pleasure, her inner muscles gripping him continuously. An orgasm like she had never felt before raced through her body. Her inner muscles closed hard, the feel of Demariak inside of her intensifying. He thrust hard into her, his fast repetitive motions never ending. His balls continued to slap against her clit. Orgasm after orgasm exploded inside of her. The sound of their combined moans reverberated throughout the room. The sound of their sweat-soaked skin slapping together heightened her pleasure. Her pussy wept to be filled. His big arm reached around, gripping one of her breasts in his big, sweaty palm. He pinched the nipple between forefinger and thumb, and tweaked it. The pleasure traveled down to her belly button and straight to her clit. His massive body tensed. Hot pulsing jets of his semen coated her insides. The pulsing seemed to go on forever, and soon after Demariak pulled out of her.

She collapsed on the bed, and closed her eyes and sighed in contentment. Every cell in her tingled, the very tips of her fingers and toes numb from the aftershocks. Demariak got off the bed and went into the bathroom. The sound of water splashing came from the darkened room. The bed dipped next to her as he brought her body flush with his. Mena rested her head on his bicep, loving the feel of his hand stroking her arm. He softly whispered to her in his language.

"Demariak?" He continued to rub her arm in a soothing way.

"Yes, *thalla*?"

"You didn't use a condom, and I'm not on the pill, so that could cause some major problems." Speaking in a lazy, half-asleep tone, she knew she should be more worried. Her body was completely satisfied, every cell pulsating sexual fulfillment. She really didn't care at the moment. It had been more of an idle thought than anything else. Tomorrow was another day, and the severity of the consequences would hit her then.

"Our females are only fertile when the moons are at their fullest. Unless two members of my tribe wish to conceive young together, we do not have sexual intercourse during the high moons. We don't have condoms as you have on your dimension because our females are fertile only during that time. Any other time there is no chance for young to be produced."

His voice spoke next to her ear and sent shivers down her spine.

"Well, I'm not from your dimension, so those rules don't apply to me. What about diseases? I mean, I don't have anything, and I'm not implying you do, but well, you know. I'm just wondering." The more she thought about it, the more worried she got. Not because she thought of all of the negative things that could possibly come out of this, but what if she got pregnant? That would make this whole situation clearly real and... permanent.

"*Thalla*, please do not worry. We do not have diseases of a sexual nature here. We are different from beings in your dimension. Our bodies cannot get or carry disease like that."

"Well, what about me? I can get pregnant whether your moons are at their fullest or not. Can your, you know, sperm get me pregnant?" Her face got hot from her question. She waited for what seemed like forever before he answered.

"I truly don't know the answer to that, *thalla*. Since I have been leader of this tribe, we have not encountered someone from your dimension before to know how that works."

"But you know English. If you have never seen someone from my dimension, then how can you speak it?" She turned and looked into his eyes.

"We are taught it when we are very young. When my grandfather led the *ZorZack* tribe, they encountered males and females from your dimension. But there are no records of sexual relations with the females that could have resulted in young being conceived. I really don't know if it is possible." Stroking her hair, Demariak stared down at her and lightly kissed her on the lips.

That was the last thing she felt before she succumbed to sleep.

Chapter Ten

The following three weeks flew by for Mena, and she actually enjoyed her stay. She spent more time with the females of the ZorZack tribe, learning their customs. She picked up on some of their language, mainly common phrases they used daily. She was still getting used to the clothing the woman wore, or, more so, the attire they didn't wear. Kitty was still pissed about the whole situation, and Mena couldn't blame her. If she hadn't found comfort with Demariak, if she hadn't felt so welcome and accepted, she would have felt the same way as Kitty.

She tried to include Kitty in the tribe's activities. She tried to find something that would interest Kitty, whether it be making crafts with the females or helping to cook the meals. Kitty showed no interest in any of those, though. More often than not, she would find Kitty in the garden, staring off and humming to herself. She tried to talk to her about it, but there wasn't anything that could make the situation better for Kitty. She was stuck in her own despair, her sadness so strong it encompassed her whole being. Mena's heart broke every time she saw this. How could she stay here when her dearest friend was so miserable? That was the growing conflict that waged war inside of Mena every day.

Mena thought something would have happened between Kitty and Keirak by now, a friendship at the least. She hoped at least a friendship with him would have brought Kitty out of the hole she had crawled into. She tried to be there for Kitty, to show her comfort in this difficult time, but more often than not, Kitty retreated to her room and shut the world out of what she felt. Everything Mena said fell on deaf ears.

As much as she wanted to comfort Kitty and make her feel comfortable, Mena couldn't help but enjoy her time in *Dimi of the Seven Moons*. She felt guilty for the happiness she felt when Kitty felt such sadness. This place made sense to her, as if it was the exact match to the puzzle piece of her life. Inside of her, her heart knew this was where she belonged.

She had tried to explain everything to Kitty, tried to tell her what Demariak said about this world. Kitty was stubborn, not wanting to hear any of it. Mena knew Kitty was angry with her, knew deep down she was upset that Mena had found happiness here. She tried every day, though, to explain everything to Kitty. It became a little better each day, with Kitty actually staying in the same room and hearing her out. Once Mena had gotten Kitty's attention, she told her about how the portal showed up once a month. Kitty immediately calmed down and started to try and plot out their escape plan. Mena saw the wheels moving inside Kitty's head. Her sadness and despair were replaced with determination and concentration. That's all Kitty wanted to talk about. She participated in more activities. She helped with the cooking and even made dozens of baskets with the females. Mena knew it wasn't because she had become acclimated to this new place. She knew how Kitty's brain worked, and she knew this was all part of her plan. Kitty was gathering as much information as she could about *Dimi of the Seven Moons* and the *ZorZack tribe*. Mena had asked Kitty why she was so interested all of a sudden, after so long being angry. Kitty became instantly defensive and denied it, even proclaiming she was just curious about her "new home". Mena of course knew better.

Mena would be lying if she said she didn't miss her home. She missed the little comforts Earth offered. On days when the rain fell down, she sat by the bay window, just watching the droplets slide off the glass. She missed food and her bedroom. All those little things that she took for granted. She would feel homesick, but then Demariak would smile at her and her heart lit up. Rain drops and comfort food could be replaced but the love of Demariak couldn't.

Demariak showed her around the tribe's territory, which Mena learned was built right into a huge mountain. The tribe's territory went from the top of the mountain to hundreds of feet below it. He told her their tribe wasn't as large as it had been back when his grandfather and great-grandfather ruled. Even though they lived in such a large area, most of their people were killed during missions outside of the tribe.

Spending more and more time with him, Mena saw a side of Demariak she knew he never showed anyone else. His thoughtfulness touched her heart. He brought her exotic-looking flowers for no reason, telling her how beautiful she was, how much he cared for her. It amazed her to think that such a large and powerful man could be so affectionate and caring. Was she actually falling for him?

Oh, who are you kidding, Mena? You love the guy.

Even though she loved Demariak, she knew it would be impossible to stay with him. She had a home that she missed, a job that she needed. Aside from Kitty, she didn't have a family. It killed her to know she couldn't stay with him, but Kitty was more important to her. She couldn't abandon her only family, even if that meant it would break her heart.

Walking with Kitty toward a room that resembled a garden, Mena once again listened to Kitty map out their escape.

"Okay, so if I calculated this right, in seven days there will be another portal. I just don't know the exact location. I say we make a break for it in six days. That way we can trek our way back to where it was when we went through it. Hopefully, it will be there again."

Watching Kitty, Mena couldn't get rid of the feeling that Kitty's ramblings resembled those of a mad scientist. Kitty had never been the one to map stuff out and try to find solutions to problems. She almost thought Kitty had lost her mind. Walking into the garden,

Kitty still talked as Mena pulled her down next to her on a stone bench. The garden was beautiful, with the most unusual flowers she had ever seen. The room was carved into a circle instead of the traditional square shape. A large fountain sat in the center of the room. Within the fountain, a large flower that looked like a daffodil and a tulip mixed together was carved out of white stone. The high ceiling gave the room an open feeling. The walls were, once again, carved with the tribal designs and wording. Mena came to find out it was the *ZorZack* tribe's ancient text. The floor and the walls had the same smooth stone as everywhere else. The flowers all around made it the most beautiful room.

Thankfully they were all alone, because no matter where they went, Keirak always seemed to be within eye distance of Kitty. Mena started to get a little creeped out by the whole thing, but Demariak assured her it was for Kitty's well-being. Mena practically begged Demariak to call his guard dog off of Kitty so they could have some *girl time* together. After a good, healthy debate, she got her way. Grabbing Kitty's hand, she waited until Kitty realized it and stopped talking.

"What?" Looking frustrated, Kitty stared at her.

"Kit, I know you want to go home. Hell, I miss the place, too, but I am getting worried about you. Nonstop you have been talking about escaping. I mean, this place isn't so bad, right? What if I agree with you, and we go off into the jungle or whatever the hell it is called? What then? Didn't you hear me when I told you Demariak says it is not safe to travel at night?"

"Mena, don't be stupid. That's just their scare tactic to get you to stay. If I didn't know better, I'd think you wanted to stay here!" She stared at Mena and had long since taken her hand back.

"Don't be silly. Of course I want to go home. I just think we need to be smart about it. Why don't we just ask Demariak and his men to help us find it?"

Yeah right, you don't want to go home. Don't lie to Kitty and yourself. Could you really leave Demariak after knowing how you feel about him? No, probably not.

Shaking her head to clear it, she watched as Kitty rolled her eyes.

"Come on, they are so not going to help us. We are on our own in this. This isn't our world. We are not like them. We need to get back to our home, to all of our friends and family." Kitty's eyes became glossy, her tears threatening to overflow.

She wasn't about to debate with Kitty that nothing waited for her back home. Her job was entry level, and she really didn't like her coworkers. Her family was non-existent, and she really had no friends. Kitty was her family—her only real friend. She knew there would be an argument if she pointed that fact out, and she wasn't about to beef it out with Kitty. She couldn't help the sadness that overwhelmed her when she saw the fat tears roll down Kitty's cheeks. Kitty had many friends, a job she loved, and men that would kill just to go on a date with her. She was going places in her life and had much more to lose if she stayed here. It killed Mena to leave Demariak, but how could she turn her back on her best friend? "Oh, Kit, please don't cry. You're right. We'll find a way out of this. I just think we should be smart about it."

"We will. Just let me think about it some more."

She sniffled and wiped her nose, her face instantly brightening at the prospect of them leaving. She was torn between the friend she held so dear and the man she loved. Her heart broke at the thought of leaving him.

It's for the best. It's for Kitty.

* * * *

The next couple of days took its toll on Mena. She felt awkward to say the least. The more time she spent with Demariak, the harder it got to leave with Kitty. There were times when she thought he might suspect something, especially when Kitty and she would meet in the garden. She would insist on being alone for their girl time. The look on his face spoke volumes, even though he would say nothing. Every day it got harder and harder. Every time they made love, a piece of her heart broke a little more when she would think about going back home. It was during those intimate times that she would think about what she was giving up. When he would gently whisper to her and tell her how special she was to him, she just wanted to cry. Many times she wanted to confess, to tell him everything. She refrained every time, though, not wanting to betray Kitty when she obviously hurt deep inside.

Kitty would hatch more plans on how to escape, and it would make Mena more ill every time. Then she would look at Kitty, see the hope reflected on her face, and push her selfishness to the side.

It being the day that Kitty and she planned to leave, she tried to act as normal as possible. Her nerves were shot and her heart ached. She felt nauseated by the whole thing, and several times she wanted to tell Kitty she wouldn't go with her. If something happened to Kitty out there, she wouldn't be able to forgive herself. Maybe one day she would come across the portal again and things could be different. An impossible thing to hope for, she knew. She kept in the back of her mind that the possibility that they wouldn't be able to find the portal was huge. Everything that could go wrong bounced around in her head until it pounded.

* * * *

It was a long, quiet walk back to Demariak's chamber, which she now claimed as her own. They walked side by side, the silence a heavy weight between them. They ate a nice meal with all of the warriors and women laughing and joking. Kitty of course clammed up during the whole meal, not even touching the food. Mena wanted to leave when the *deyada berries* came out. Demariak was very quiet himself during the meal, his jaw ticking at times and his face in a scowl. She and Kitty made plans to meet in the garden later that night. It was all she could think about and was not even able to enjoy the wonderful food in front of her. She picked at the food, more playing with it than anything else. She hardly spoke to Kitty during the meal, both of them making eye contact as they left for the evening. She stopped and placed one hand on the wall and one hand on her stomach as a wave of nausea overtook her.

Calm down. You're letting your nerves get the better of you.

"*Thalla*, are you all right? You seem a little ill." Taking hold of her waist, he watched her with concern on his face.

She cleared her throat, and righted herself. "I'm fine, really. My stomach is just a little bit upset." She tried to sound like she told the truth. She looked into his face and gave a weak smile. Her eyes went wide, and she yelped as Demariak scooped her into his arms and carried her to the bedroom. "What are you doing? I can walk fine."

"I think our tribe's healing woman should see you. You might be getting sick, and things here can make you so ill, you die quickly without warning."

She swallowed roughly, knowing she couldn't tell him it was just her nerves about her plans for tonight. "I'm fine, really. It's getting late, and I don't want to make someone come all the way over here when it's just an upset stomach." Demariak lowered her to the ground and opened the bedroom door. She walked inside with Demariak's arm loose around her waist. He turned her, his big, warm hand caressing her face.

"Okay, *thalla*, I will not call the healer tonight, but tomorrow will you see her—in the morning?"

Closing her eyes, she felt him caress her cheek. His hand moved to the back of her head, bringing her head to his chest. She could feel the strong beat of his heart and had to fight back the tears that threatened to spill. Clearing her throat, she kept her head on his chest and rested her hand on his shoulder.

"Okay, Demariak, I'll see her in the morning if it will make you feel better." Looking up at him, Mena saw the troubled expression marring his face.

"Oh, *thalla*. Do you realize how dear you are to me? I want to pick only the most beautiful flowers for you, and even though your beauty outshines them, my heart skips a beat when I see the happiness in your eyes at seeing them. I want to spend forever and always with you. If you were no longer near me, my heart would shatter into a million pieces, and I could never repair it. I love you with every piece of my being."

Tears fell down her cheek. Mena cleared her throat and looked away. She knew she should have said something, but she was just too stunned. She couldn't believe what Demariak had just told her.

Chapter Eleven

"Do you not care for me as well, *thalla*?" Sorrow filled his voice.

She met his gaze, wanting to assure him. "Oh yes, Demariak. I love you so much it hurts!"

He pulled her body into a crushing embrace. "This is good, Thalla, very good. So then you will not leave this night?"

Mena gasped and pulled away. *How had he known about the plan?*

"How did you know? I mean, I thought I hid it so well!" She looked into his face with wide eyes, and felt her face flush.

"*Thalla*, even though I told you I would give you and Kitty privacy, I always made sure one of my warriors was within hearing distance of you. I myself never stayed close to you because I didn't want to betray your trust personally, but I felt if it wasn't me, it was different. I am sorry to have betrayed your trust, but I couldn't take any chances with you. Even though we are inside of this great mountain, and it is guarded like a fortress, there can still be hidden dangers. I could not leave what is so precious to me unprotected."

She didn't forget about the horrid creatures he had told her about when she first arrived. Every time she thought about leaving, sharp teeth and wicked claws flashed through her mind. Kitty knew the dangers. Mena made sure to remind her of those dangers whenever they spoke. Of course nothing seemed to discourage Kitty from leaving. Even though Mena was angry that he had people spying on her and Kitty's conversations, she couldn't help but feel flattered that he would protect her so much. The love she felt for him grew so much at that moment that her eyes watered. "You know I should be so upset that you lied to me, but just knowing you didn't want anything to hurt me has to be the sweetest thing. But know that I am still pissed at you!" She tried to look mad and saw the corner of his mouth twitch in amusement.

"Oh, great queen, please forgive me," he said, bowing his head as if she were royalty.

She slapped him lightly on the shoulder. "Oh, quit with the queen stuff, you smartass."

A smile covered his face as he brought his head up. He took her face between both his big hands and kissed her lightly on the lips. "Mena, my love, will you stay with me in my kingdom and be my queen to rule beside me for the rest of our days?"

Her mouth fell open as he took both her hands in his, got down on both his knees, and bowed his head to her hands. "Are you serious? You don't think this is too fast? I mean, how will your people react?" Would his tribe accept her? She truly was ecstatic about his proposal, but a little voice inside her head told her to be cautious. "What if they don't like me?"

"They already love you, Mena. Can't you see that?"

His face was lit up with a smile, and she let out her own smile. She just hoped everything fell into place and that she didn't screw up. This was what a girl waited for, wasn't it? To be proposed to by a king, to have him bowing before her.

"Oh, my beautiful one, nothing would please me more than if you would rule by my side and someday carry my young within you." He looked up at her and kissed her hands and waited for her to answer.

She wanted to say *yes*—scream it, in fact—because of how happy she was. Of course, Kitty's face popped into her mind at that exact moment. "What about Kitty? I mean, she is really determined to find the portal and get back home. What are we going to do about that?" She bit her lip, as Demariak brought his large body to its fullest height, scooped her up—yet again—and carried her over to the bed.

"Fear not, my love. If she likes, we will work our hardest to make her comfortable here."

"You don't understand. She wants to find that portal and leave."

"I fear that it might be a hopeless journey, because the next time it appears, it may be on the other side of my world. I must admit, though, I think Keirak has taken a fondness to your dear friend."

He obviously didn't know Kitty very well. She wouldn't be placated by anything she was told. Mena shook her head, not about to tell him that unless Kitty went home she wouldn't be happy. What should she do? She was torn between the two people who meant the most to her.

He smiled and sat her on the bed, turned, and walked to a black stone table that had a small, white, jewel-encrusted box on it. He moved away from her, and she couldn't help but notice how his body moved with the gracefulness and power of a predator. The tattoo that covered his back enhanced his air of leadership, making his whole persona scream danger. Her sex seeped instantly, and her nipples hardened at the simple way he moved. He picked up the box and brought it over to her.

The box fit in the length of her palm. It had beautiful engravings etched into the wood. She marveled at how the candlelight picked up on the facets of the white jewels, making a rainbow of color wash the room. "What is this?" Not bothering to look up at him, she ran her hand over the jewels and the small latch that kept it closed.

"In this box, if you choose to stay by my side, holds a treasure that doesn't compare to what you mean to me. So, my sweetness, I will ask you again, will you stand by my side as my queen always and be the only one who holds my heart forever?"

She looked up from the box as he once again got on both his knees and placed his hands on her hips. He stroked her hips, caressing her body in a way that set a fire inside of her. He gently took the box from her and opened it to reveal its contents.

Inside the red silk-lined box, a beautiful necklace lay on the material like an offering. She watched in awe as he plucked the necklace out of the box to hold it up in front of her. The length was so long, it would no doubt reach her belly button. Hundreds of tiny strands made up the necklace. Jewels upon jewels covered the delicate strands. The candlelight caught the jewels, casting a rainbow across its confines. She took the necklace from him, and loved the feel of its weight in her hands.

She looked at him and saw how intently he stared at her. "It's so beautiful."

"It doesn't compare to you, my sweet. This *dencha,* as we call it, has been passed down from each queen that has ruled beside the king of my tribe."

He lifted his hand, and lightly stroked her face, a look of anxiety and trepidation covering his features.

"Oh, Demariak, I want to be with you always, but what am I supposed to do about Kitty? She's my best friend, and she wants to go home so badly."

"If she truly wants to go home, then I will dispatch my men to go in search for it. I can't say how long it will take to find it, though. Its location changes every time. I feel, though, that she could be truly happy here. She could find a loyal mate, make a family for herself, if she gave it a chance."

He took the necklace from her, reaching behind her neck to clasp it together. She looked down at the necklace, noticing how nicely it covered her. She looked up at him and idly ran her fingers over the necklace. The metal felt cool beneath her fingers, the jewels' texture rasping over her skin. She wrapped her arms around his neck and yelled *yes*, that she had never wanted anything more in her life than to stay with him, be with him forever.

"Oh, Demariak, make love to me. Make me your queen."

Chapter Twelve

They made soft, sweet love together. Not rushing it, just two bodies loving each other. He was so gentle with her, making sure she knew how much he loved her. Her body pressed close to his, she stared at the intricate etchings on the ceiling and couldn't help but shake her head at how her life had changed so drastically. Just days ago she had actually contemplated leaving the strong powerful man who lay beside her. She loved him so powerfully, with an emotion that she had never experienced before. He made her feel beautiful, smart, and sexy. He showered her with gentleness and kindness, loved her above all. She turned to her side and looked at his sleeping form. She brought her hand up to his hair and ran her fingers through the short, silky pieces.

"What is it my sweet? Something bothers you?" She smiled as he brought his arms around her waist and pulled her body closer to his. Laying her head on his bicep, she wrapped her arm around his waist, running her hands up and down the hard muscles of his back.

"Nothing. I've just been thinking about how foolish I was to even think that I could have a life without you."

His hand ran lazy circles along her back, eliciting goose bumps on her flesh. "What shall we do with Kitty, my love?"

"She wants to meet late tonight so we can make our escape. She thinks we will find the portal and said that tonight will be the night it shows itself." Biting her lower lip, she sat up and looked at him. He watched her with those devilish blue eyes that made her wet for him in an instant. "I'll just meet her as planned and talk her out of it. I'll remind her about what we could encounter out there. She's hard-headed though, only wanting to do what she feels like. At the very least, I will talk her out of leaving tonight. I will tell her you offered to have your men go on a search for the portal. Hopefully that will placate her enough to stay."

Picking up her hand, Demariak brought it to his chest and breathed in deeply. "Promise me that you won't let her talk you into leaving with her tonight." He sat up, the look on his face intense and powerful.

"What?"

He looked mad almost, even after she told him what he meant to her. "*Thalla*, I will tell you this: if you run, I will track you. I will stop at nothing until I have you again. There is nothing on my world or yours that can keep me from you."

She was surprised at the excitement that spiked inside of her. The look of pure determination and possession on his face made a strong burst of arousal course through her. "Is that right?" She was playing with fire, she knew, but it was oh so fun. He lifted an eyebrow, a look of surprise momentarily flashing across his face. *I guess no one has ever questioned him before.* She smiled, knowing he cared so much for her that he wouldn't let anything or anyone stand in his way to get to her.

"You don't have to look so scary when you say that, damn it." She got off the bed and stood, turning toward him and placing her hands on her hips. "Have you not been listening to anything I've said? All the stuff I told you about what you mean to me? I am not going anywhere, so don't worry! Anyways, if I did decide to leave, where would I go?"

"Mena, love, I just wanted to let you know where I stand on the whole situation with you. I trust you with all of my being, but if something happened to you, I couldn't handle it. And I fear for anyone who is within my wrath. Go talk with Kitty. I will be here when you return… ready to service my queen."

He wagged his eyebrows, and she couldn't hold back the laugh that came out of her. Just when she thought she had Demariak figured out, he surprised her once again. She picked up the black silk robe and covered her body. She shivered at the sensuality of the fabric as it slid along her skin. She gave him a light kiss on the cheek and silently headed out the door to meet up with Kitty.

* * * *

Hours passed before she was supposed to meet Kitty, but she figured she would just go to Kitty's room and talk to her about the whole situation. She stood in front of Kitty's door and lightly tapped on it. She didn't hear an answer so she slightly opened the door. Kitty ran around the room, shoving things into burlap-type sacks.

"What are you doing?" Entering the room, Mena closed the door and walked toward Kitty.

"What? Oh, Mena, it's just you. What are you doing here? We aren't supposed to meet for another couple of hours." Kitty threw more items in the bags, and Mena caught glimpses of different types of fruit and vegetables along with clothing and jugs of water.

"What are you going to do with all of that stuff? You have enough packed for an army." Walking up to one of the sacks, Mena pulled it open to reveal knives and other small weapons she saw the warriors use. She arched a brow at the weapons and looked up at Kitty who now sat on the bed tying up the sacks. "What's with all the weapons?"

"Well, if we're going out into that hell hole again, I want to be prepared. I have been sneaking off with these things when no one was looking and stashing them away behind the bed."

When Kitty glanced up at her, Mena knew she probably had a what-the-hell-are-you-thinking look on her face. "How did you get all of this stuff without anyone knowing? I thought Keirak was always by you?" Mena knew Keirak kept a close eye on Kitty, and she was amazed Kitty managed to collect all of it.

"Well, Keirak has to sleep and do other bodily functions, so, that's when I got everything."

"What do you plan on doing with weapons you don't even know how to use?" Mena sat on the bed and picked up a small knife nestled in one of the bags.

"I've been practicing with them before bed. I think I've got the hang of them. I have to be on alert, though, because that watch dog, Keirak, seems to be always right behind me." Kitty took a deep breath, and finally tied up the last of the sacks and slumped back on the bed. "I'm glad you're here now though. I was going to come for you early anyways since I want to leave right away. We need all the extra time we can get if we are going to find the portal." Kitty got up, walked over to the door, and opened it. She stuck her head out, looked both ways, then shut the door silently and walked back to the bed, sitting on the edge.

She inhaled deeply, and let out a long sigh as she looked back at Mena. They stared at each other for what seemed like hours.

Mena placed her hand on Kitty's shoulder, trying to think of how to best present her case. Before she even said anything, she saw Kitty's brows furrow over her eyes and a frown set in.

"Mena, if you're about to say what I think you're going to say, then save it!" Kitty moved farther on the bed, making Mena's hand drop with a soft thump.

"Calm down, you don't even know what I'm going to say." She didn't want to start off the conversation with Kitty like this. She hoped deep down inside that Kitty might accept the idea of, at the very least, waiting to find the portal. Standing up, Kitty paced the width of the bed and then stopped right in front of Mena with her arms hanging loosely to her sides.

"This is about you staying right? And let me guess..." She placed a finger by her mouth and tapped lightly. "You have fallen madly in love with that beast of a man, are planning on living happily ever after, and popping out a couple of babies?" Going over to the bed, she sat next to Mena and placed her hands on top of Mena's. "Mena, listen to me. This Demariak," closing her eyes and shaking her head, she looked as if she were in pain, "has brainwashed you. Don't you want to go home? Sleep in your own bed in your own house? I miss all of those things."

Mena thought over what Kitty said. She shook her head, not even knowing what to say. "Kitty, look, you are all I have. I don't have any family, no real friends, and my job sucks. If I were here alone, then yes, I would want to go back because you weren't here with me. I know I am being selfish about my feelings, Kitty. I see how unhappy you are here, and it kills me, it truly does. You're my best friend, my sister—you know I would do anything for you. I can't stand to see this depression that has settled into you. It breaks my heart. I won't lie and say I miss home, because, to be honest, this feels more like my home. I truly feel like this is where I belong." She took a deep breath, tears starting to crest in her eyes. "I love you too much, though, and if you really want to leave, then I can't let you do it alone."

How had things turned out like this? Mena looked down at their overlapping hands, a tear falling from her eye and dropping on her skin.

"I haven't been blind, Mena. I've seen how much you love this place, how you feelings have grown for Demariak. I feel lost here, though, like I am just floating along, watching as life passes me by. How can I make you come with me when I know what you would be missing, what your life could become?"

They both started to cry, and Mena pulled Kitty into a hug. "I can't let you go alone, though. I would die if something happened to you out there." Mena had the full intention of trying to coax Kitty into staying, but that of course wasn't how things worked out. She looked into Kitty's grief-stricken face, and it twisted Mena's heart. If Kitty would just wait, at least so Demariak and his men could help them, this journey wouldn't be so dangerous.

"Demariak told me he would have his men help you find a portal; you just have to give him some time to get everything together."

Kitty laughed sarcastically. "I'm sure he would, Mena, but how long do you think that would take? If I don't go now and at least try to find it, I may never have the opportunity to again. I need to do this, Mena. I don't fit here. I have to do this on my own. I can't stay here waiting for them to help me go home."

"Kitty, please, I love you. You're my family. Let's think things through, please. You know what kinds of dangers are out there, things we can't even comprehend. There are creatures, monsters out there that won't hesitate to rip you apart. I'm not going to try any longer to convince you to stay here. I will leave with you if that's what you truly want, but please let's have the warriors help us."

Shaking her head in what could only be anger and distaste, Kitty picked up a few of the bags. She had too many, though, and Kitty was forced to select only a few to carry.

"You know, Mena, it's clear you love this place, that you believe everything they tell you. I am not so trusting though. I can't leave my fate in the hands of men whom I don't trust. I haven't formed any attachment here. You're the only reason I didn't leave the very first night. You've found your peace here. I just feel like an outsider looking in. I am, though, aren't I, an outsider?" Mena started to respond, but Kitty cut her off with a wave of her hand. "It makes no difference, really. I mean, I kind of knew deep down that you would stay, but I hoped I was wrong."

Mena didn't know what to say. She couldn't just let her walk away but she couldn't make her stay. Mena watched, her mind blank, as Kitty grabbed what she could and headed out the door without a single look back.

Chapter Thirteen

Kitty walked out of the room, with Mena trailing behind her. She wasn't heartless. She knew how much Mena loved this place, how much she loved Demariak. She would have left by herself, would have said goodbye to Mena if she really wanted to stay. It hurt her to see the sadness that overtook Mena's whole body as she trailed after her. She didn't even bother telling Mena to stay because she knew it would fall on deaf ears. She was secretly happy that Mena was leaving with her, and that simple emotion is what made her feel like a piece of shit. She was being selfish, and she knew it, but this place was not for her. She just hoped that once they finally did get back home, it wouldn't take Mena long to forget about all of this—if she ever did. As much as she hated this place, she did admit there had been a few good points. She learned a lot of different and interesting things and met some nice people, but she wanted desperately to go home. She didn't belong in this world, didn't fit in. She missed her boring life back home, her regular-sized bedroom with the blue star drapes and the matching bedspread. She missed her friends and family, even missed the annoying neighbor kids who liked to be extra loud early in the mornings. Walking quickly down the long, white-stoned hallway, she looked over her shoulder. Mena walked behind her, a couple of bags hanging from her shoulders. Mena attempted a sincere smile, but it fell very short of its mark. The sadness and worry that creased her beautiful features overshadowed everything else.

"Here, I'll lead us out. You don't even know where to go."

She smiled at Mena and adjusted one of the bags hanging from her shoulder. "Actually I had a feeling you would end up changing your mind and want to stay here, so during the time I've been here, I found a way out myself."

"Clever, aren't you?"

Mena couldn't believe how this all had played out. Kitty turned back around and made her way down the corridor. Mena didn't know what else to do but follow her. She wanted to talk to Kitty more, at least try to change her mind. Temptation nagged at her to yell for Demariak, but really, what would he do? Hold Kitty down and make her stay? She couldn't do that to Kitty, and she certainly didn't want to cause problems for anyone. No, the best thing to do was shut up and get out of here quickly.

Kitty walked through the tunnels like she lived here, knowing every twist and turn. Mena followed Kitty past a sharp curve and was greeted with a small hallway made up of dull-looking gray stone. It looked nothing like any of the other hallways, its dinginess making it appear drab.

Mena was so confused and had no idea where they were. She turned around in a small circle, trying to see more than just plain, gray rock surrounding her. The small space barely had any lighting, only a soft glow from the hallway to illuminate it. She heard a light scraping sound and turned toward Kitty. Kitty stood by the farthest part of the wall, her fingers running over the stone. She pushed in a piece of the wall, and the stone easily moved.

The small square-shaped piece looked like the rest of the wall and was only a little bit bigger than Kitty's hand. Mena would have never noticed it if she had stumbled by this place on her own, and it made her wonder how Kitty could have possibly found it.

"What are you doing?" She walked closer to Kitty, watching as she pushed the square-shaped stone in until it wouldn't move anymore. Mena jumped back as the wall in front of them slid silently to the side, revealing another cave-like entrance.

"Kitty, what the hell just happened, and how did you know about that?"

"I followed one of the men one day, on one of the rare occasions I was actually free of my watch dog. Anyways, he came to this small alcove. I watched from behind one of the shadowed corners as he put his hand on the wall and made the wall open up. It leads outside."

Mena walked closer and ran her hand over the cold wall, expecting a trap door to spring open.

"Once I figured out how to do it, I tried every day to get it to open up."

"How did you come here every day without anyone knowing?"

"You mean without Keirak knowing?"

Mena nodded, her attention still on the gray stone.

"Every day, around the same time, Keirak would go to practice with his weapons. I followed him the first couple of times, kind of curious as to what he was doing. He's pretty good, really good actually. Anyways, those are the times I came over here."

"How do you know what's on the other side?"

Mena stepped back, her eyes on Kitty.

"I watched the men open it. There is a cave on the other side, and beyond that, well, I don't know. The outside I assume."

"Oh."

Fear became thick inside of Mena. Not knowing what lay on the other side was worse than knowing what greeted them very soon.

"I thought someone actually caught me once. I ran to the alcove one night and tried to open the damned thing again when I heard footsteps coming. I dashed into a corner before I was caught." She walked through the opened stone door, and Mena had no choice but to follow her. She couldn't let her just leave and possibly get injured—or worse.

"Kitty, please. This is really not a good idea."

Kitty stopped and turned around. "Listen, just go back, Mena." She shook her head, turning back around and walking again.

Mena didn't bother saying anything else. She just hoped Kitty came to her senses once they finally left the cave.

"So anyways, I ran into the corner because I heard someone coming—turned out to be that beast of a man, Keirak."

Mena agreed with Kitty there. Keirak was a hulking man, almost as tall as Demariak, and certainly not lacking any of the muscles.

"There is no way he could have seen me because of the darkened corner. I even crouched between two large boulders to make sure he didn't see me." Adjusting the bags on her shoulder, Kitty let out a big sigh. "So anyway, I am crammed up against these rocks, and I hear him making his way toward the wall, no doubt about to open it. I peeked my head around the corner, making sure I was still in the shadows, when I see his hand go up to that invisible stone square." She adjusted the straps of the bags once again and went on with her story.

"As his hand was just about to press down on the stone, he stopped in mid air, and slowly turned toward the corner I huddled behind. My heart beat so fast I thought for sure he could hear it. I willed myself to be calm, to slow my breathing. I didn't want him to be able to sense me, but it seemed like an unbeatable task to accomplish. I thought he caught me. I heard some more men walk into the alcove, and, thankfully, that distracted him, or he hadn't sensed me."

Knitting her eyebrows, Mena thought it was funny how Kitty worded that. *He couldn't sense me?* Not about to even go there, she saw Kitty look over her shoulder and look her in the eye.

"Oh, you didn't know, did you?"

She walked faster toward Kitty, who picked up her pace. She lightly grabbed hold of Kitty's arm and stopped her, which made Kitty turn around with a scowl on her face.

"What are you doing? I want to get the hell out of here, and you are just dragging it out! Are you waiting for your backup or something?" Huffing to herself, Kitty's face got a little pink, a sure sign of her mounting anger.

"I'm not waiting for any backup, Kitty. Stop acting like this!" Her voice rose so she willed herself to calm down. "First of all, I am only acting like this because I care about you and don't want anything bad to happen to you. Second of all, you're being stubborn, and I hate that quality in you!" She watched as Kitty's lips quirked up in amusement, but then she quickly hid it. "I want to know what you mean about him *sensing* you. That is a weird way of putting something. I mean, you make it sound like they're animals or something."

Kitty dropped to the ground and let out a sigh and faced Mena again. "I'm not surprised your little boyfriend didn't tell you, but since you have decided to stay here, I am going to lay it all out for you."

After what seemed like forever, Mena waved her hand in a gesture for Kitty to go on. "I sat in the fountain room one day, watching the water come down the wall when I overheard a deep voice. I heard children's voices so I went to the next room and peeked through the door. About ten children sat in a circle around this massive man. It reminded me of story time or something. The children were little boys, and the instructor, I guess is what you would call him, told the boys how to spot their enemy and hunt them. The man went into detail about using their sense of smell to track their prey down and so on. I mean, Mena, these people can *smell* when you're scared, angry, or… aroused." Flushing brightly, Kitty turned away for a moment before she continued

"They can see at night just like some kind of panther or something. I don't have to remind you about their strength or size. They are far from human, and a big part of the reason I am leaving is because that scares the shit out of me." Flipping a lock of hair over her shoulder, she continued. "I mean, who knows what else these… *men* can do!"

Kitty must be wrong. Mena knew Demariak wasn't like other men. They were on another dimension, so of course things would be different than what they knew. Even though Kitty talked about them like they should be beasts to fear, Demariak was so gentle with her. He always went out of his way to make her not frightened of him. No matter what the difference, she knew Demariak would never let anything happen to her. If that meant she needed to get used to supernatural powers, so to speak, well then, she could live with that. Kitty didn't give her a chance to respond. She just picked up her bags and shook her head. She walked again, the subject being completely dropped. Mena looked ahead and could see the glow of the night.

"Kitty, I really don't think this is a good idea." The closer they got to the mouth of the cave, the more she felt tingles go down her spine. She didn't feel right and knew this situation wasn't going to be good.

"Go back, Mena. I don't expect you to go with me, and, honestly, all you have been trying to do is talk me out of it, which you know is a lost cause."

True, Mena knew how stubborn she was, but still she couldn't just watch her walk into the unknown. She should have called for Demariak.

Chapter Fourteen

They walked through the mouth of the cave, the cool air wafting over their faces. Mena turned and looked behind her, the cave just a small opening in a huge mountain. The mountain took up her entire view, going on for miles and miles on either side of her. Turning back around, she could make out the moons above her through a break in the trees. They both just stood there for a minute, looking around at the jungle and all of the shadows that could be hiding unknown threats. Their surroundings held an eerie silence. Not even the rustle of animals gave any sound.

"Kitty, let's go back inside. I mean it. Can't you feel how wrong this is? I am not going to just leave you by yourself out here, so don't even say it." Mena looked down at her hands, realizing she was twisting her fingers together. She looked up at Kitty, whose hands tightly gripped the bag's straps.

"If I just start to walk, it'll be fine. The darkness always makes everything look scary." Not even looking back, Kitty slowed her pace as they made their way into the unknown darkness.

Oh, hell. Mena did not want to go out there. She had told Demariak she wouldn't leave, that she would be right back. She could run back and get him, but she wouldn't leave Kitty by herself.

Bad idea, this is such a bad idea!

* * * *

They walked through the bushes, only ten minutes into Kitty's little journey. They both wore the transparent dresses, and the cool air passing through the thin material made them both shiver. Mena didn't say as much, but the breeze wasn't the only thing making her shiver. Fear was at the forefront of her mind, every little sound causing her heart to pound against her ribs. As they made their way through the thick foliage, the branches whipped at her arms and legs, causing her skin to burn and throb. Their travel was slow, and Mena still tried desperately to get Kitty to turn around, but with no luck. She knew it was a lost cause, but fear coursed through her body and she did it out of instinct. A few times, Kitty stopped and looked around, seeming like she might turn back. She would then shake her head and mumble something to herself and trek on. Walking close to Kitty, Mena's eyes finally adjusted to the darkness. The light from the moon penetrated the branches, casting an ethereal silver glow around them. The breeze whistled through the branches, small twigs snapping all around them, and paranoia coated Mena's senses. Looking around, she stopped dead in her tracks and whispered Kitty's name.

"What? I swear if you're going to talk me out of it one more time, I'm going to scream. Just turn around already." Mena was vaguely aware of Kitty stopping and turning towards her, but she would not turn away from the source that held her attention. Her body shook uncontrollably, and her teeth chattered so loudly it seemed to echo off the trees. Kitty dropped the bags on the ground, the sound seeming so loud in the dead silence that surrounded them.

"Mena what's wrong?" She forced her eyes to look at Kitty, pleading with her without saying anything to be still and quiet. Kitty seemed oblivious, though, and placed a hand on her shoulder.

"Be very quiet and quit moving." She spoke through her teeth, trying to be as quiet as she could. Kitty's brow creased, and she turned around, her mouth going slack at what she saw. What stood just a few feet away from them was enormous, a beast from the darkest pits of hell.

"Oh...Holy...Hell... Mena"

* * * *

Demariak lay on the bed waiting for Mena to come back from speaking with Kitty. He knew he was stubborn and possessive, but when it came to Mena, he couldn't help himself. She did something to him, made him feel territorial and protective. She made him feel things that he never thought he could feel. She gave him strength, gave him hope, and brought out goodness in him that he didn't know he possessed.

A loud knock on his chamber door made him get out of bed. He put his leathers on before the pounding could begin again. Prowling over to the door, he ripped it open and glowered at who stood on the other side. Keirak stared at him, his face looking grim. Dread settled in Demariak's gut at Keirak's look.

"My lord, we have a problem, and it concerns the females."

Demariak didn't have to ask which females Keirak meant. Before he could even question what happened, Keirak spoke in a hard tone.

"The female, Kitty, has found the opening into the *Nenana* cave. She has managed to open it and left with your female trailing behind her."

He could feel his anger start to mount to a dangerous level. Mena swore she wouldn't leave him—told him she loved him.

"If I may speak, my lord?" At the tight nod of Demariak's head, Keirak continued. "Icezack overheard Kitty and your female speaking before they left. It is my understanding that Mena tried very hard to sway Kitty's opinion on leaving. I believe the only reason she left was to see her safe. I do not believe she truly meant to deceive you. As soon as I realized what had happened, I came to your chambers immediately to await your orders." Keirak ran a hand over his hair, mussing it up. "I would have gone after them, but by the time I found out, they were already gone. I thought it best to alert you. I await your orders."

"Why didn't Icezack stop them when he heard them speaking of leaving?"

"My lord, it is well known that Kitty didn't want to stay here. Icezack just assumed it was another one of her rants. By the time he realized what had happened, he came to me immediately."

Demariak was furious. He knew it wasn't Isaac's fault that the women left, but his anger didn't want to make that distinction. He wanted to hit something, hit it so hard he would feel his knuckles crush under the impact. He prayed to the gods that nothing would happen to Mena. Because if anything should happen to her, all would do best to steer clear of his wrath.

Keirak was his second in command and most trusted member of his tribe. Hearing him speak of Mena's intentions made him calm… slightly. Mena and Kitty had still left the safety of the mountain and the protection of the tribe. Because of that, monumental problems could arise and probably would arise.

Pacing in front of the door, he ran a hand through his short hair and sighed loudly. He could feel the anger radiating off of Keirak, and he could sense below all that anger a good dose of fear. No doubt Keirak felt the same possessive, territorial feelings toward Kitty as he felt toward Mena. He watched Keirak and the way his eyes were constantly on Kitty. He could see the lust and desire radiating off of him when she was near.

After lacing up his leather boots, he went to a hidden panel in the wall and pressed roughly on the cold stone. A loud whoosh sounded as the wall moved aside. As soon as the wall slid aside, a dim light from the back displayed a wide range of weapons.

Reaching up, he pulled down a six-foot sword and strapped it to his back with leather ties. Pulling two daggers down, he attached them on the outside of his thighs. He reached for the traditional *neeko* whip that all of the warriors in his tribe fought with. The *neeko* whip was two long, thick leather straps that had pea-sized stones sandwiched in between them. Once the whip struck an opponent, the pea-sized pebbles would crack slightly and let out toxic oil that immediately soaked into the flesh. The oil caused paralysis to the affected area. The idea was to paralyze an enemy so that one could eliminate him efficiently.

The *neeko* whip was the *ZorZack* tribe's most secret weapon in defeating their enemies. Curling the whip and attaching it to his hip, he made his way past Keirak without a sideways glance. He didn't need to say anything. Keirak would know to suit up, get the other warriors, and meet him at the entrance to the *Nenana* cave.

The only sound echoing off the stone walls was the heavy thump of his and Keirak's boots hitting the ground. The only thoughts in his head concerned Mena. The fear that he felt for her twisted in his chest, making it feel tight with pressure. Absently rubbing the spot over his heart, he could not remember a time when he feared anything. The thought of losing Mena, though, made his heart hurt and brought a dread to him the likes of which he had never felt.

Chapter Fifteen

As Mena and Kitty stood frozen in place, the only thing they could manage to do was grip onto each other's bodies. In front of them, through the thick foliage of branches and bushes, a set of white glowing eyes stared at them. The eyes were the size of baseballs and held menace in the darkness.

"K-Kitty, what is th-that?" Mena's voice trembled when she spoke.

"I don't know, but I think I should have listened to you about going back." Mena barley heard Kitty's whispered response, but neither of them wanted to draw unwanted attention. She didn't look at Kitty when she spoke, wanting only to keep her sight on the creature in front of them. She would have thought the glowing eyes might have been a trick of the light, but she could see them blinking, darkness temporarily masking their brightness.

"Kitty, we have to move very slowly and start to walk backward toward that cave again." Mena didn't know what else to say or do. The cave was at least a ten-minute walk in the other direction, and she wasn't even sure if she could remember the way. What if this thing attacks by movement, or could smell their fear? There were no other options. Either stay still and possibly get killed, or start moving and possibly get killed. As if they read each other's mind, they both moved slowly backward and to the side.

Kitty left the bags on the ground and clutched her arms as if they were a life preserver. Kitty and Mena made it only a couple of steps before Mena stepped on a twig. The sound echoed through the forest, seeming a hundred times louder then it normally would. Stopping dead in their tracks, both of them stared ahead into the glowing eyes that seemed to be getting higher. They tilted their heads back as the eyes went higher. The creature still had the darkness cloaked around its body and the light from the moons making a slash on the ground right in front of it. Staring wide-eyed, the women watched as a large, black, razor-sharp clawed foot came into the light. The claws were like swords jutting out from a four-toed, webbed foot. Bringing their eyes up, they watched in horror as the beast finally came fully into the slash of light.

Gasping at what she saw in front of them, Mena couldn't help but tremble with fright. Kitty's hands gripped her arm and shook violently. The *thing* in front of them had to be at least ten feet tall. It was all black, except for uneven lines going through it of darker shades of brown and green. It stood on two lizard-like legs and had two lizard-like arms. The claws jutted from its fingers and toes, lethal and intense-looking. On its belly tentacle-like extensions hung freely. Mena held back her gag reflex just from looking at the creature and the awful wave-like motions the tentacles made.

Her mouth went slack at seeing its face. It looked like something out of a horror movie. Its long snout and needle-sharp serrated teeth came into the slash of light, black saliva dripping on the jungle floor. It had two sets of teeth, one on the top and a set on the bottom. They shined in the moonlight with deadly intent. It hissed at them, the sound like a snake getting ready to strike.

"Oh, hell, Mena, I was wrong." Kitty cried her confession. Mena heard her softly weep and held back her own tears as she felt the prickly sensation come over her.

Damn them for leaving the bag full of weapons several feet away. Mena had known something like this would happen, and she should have stuck with her instincts. She cursed herself for not grabbing the fallen bag when they backed up. If they could find a weapon, anything within their reach, then it might give them the chance to stall for time until, hopefully, help arrived. She hoped Demariak found out that they had left. It was too much to hope for, though. He probably still lounged in their bed, awaiting her return.

Still clutching her friend, Mena slowly glanced down with only her eyes so she didn't draw any attention to herself. She tried her best to see in the little light that the moon provided. She scanned the jungle floor quickly, trying to find a weapon of some kind. She made sure to glance up every few seconds to make sure the beast hadn't advanced on them. Sure enough, the beast hadn't moved, but just kept drooling and making that disgusting hissing noise.

"Kitty, don't make a sound. I want you to follow my moves very slowly." She enunciated the last word. Mena slowly bent her knees, moving closer to the ground. She kept both eyes on the beast while she went down.

Thankfully, Kitty followed her to the ground silently. A deafening roar echoed off the jungle trees, making Mena and Kitty release their grip on each other. They covered their ears, the sound so loud it made them cringe in pain. The sound was like nothing she had ever heard before. It sounded distorted, like the thing was roaring under water. Quickly scooping up a palm-sized stone she planned on using as a weapon, Mena made sure to grab Kitty by the arm and stand back up quickly. They both became motionless again, and Mena hoped the beast hadn't noticed their movements too much.

The beast slowly slithered to them, whipping its tail from side to side and taking out chunks of tree bark in the process. It crept toward them, flicking its tongue out the same way a snake would. They didn't move, held their ground, and hoped the beast would stop. It took a couple of steps and stopped, smelling the air. It continued to hiss, drool spilling out of its mouth and landing on the razor sharp toes.

The thing can only see us when we move!

The realization surprised her, and her brain instantly started to think of a plan. The heaviness of the stone in her palm reminded her of it and gave her strength. She brought her eyes down to it, making sure to not move her head.

Making sure to barely move her mouth, she whispered, "Don't move, Kitty. That thing reacts to movement." Kitty had become silent, her breathing the only sound coming from her.

"I got that, Mena, but what are we going to do now? We can't exactly make a run for it. I have a feeling that *thing* would take one step and eat us." She said it much the same as a ventriloquist would.

The stone got warmer in Mena's hand, giving her the strength to carry on with her plan.

"I want you to follow my lead when I say so." She didn't give Kitty any time to respond. In one swift movement, she lifted her arm and threw the stone as far as she could in the opposite direction. As soon as she let go of the stone, the beast spotted it flying through the air and swung its body in that direction.

"Now!" She whispered loudly, wanting to make sure not to draw the attention of the beast back to them. Running in the other direction, they moved as fast as their legs would take them. They prayed they went in the right direction, but the darkness and their fear worked against them. The only light offered was that of the slashes of moonlight through the branches. The air felt cool on her face, and even though the leaves whipped her face and arms, she made sure to grip Kitty's hand tight and run faster.

She didn't dare look back, but then she heard the loud crunching of sticks and branches behind them. Giving in, she whipped her head over her shoulder. Kitty ran beside her, and Mena could see the fear in her eyes. She could also see the hard set of determination reflected on her face. It would have been inspirational except for the fact that another loud roar tore through the darkness, making them stumble slightly from fear.

That's when Mena saw the beast come barreling toward them with a frightening speed. Breathing deeply, Mena told Kitty to run faster and prayed they would make it in time. She was tempted to stop and hope the beast didn't sense them, but fear kept her moving. She couldn't risk it, not with the creature so close behind them.

Where are you, Demariak?

Chapter Sixteen

Demariak and a handful of his strongest warriors walked through the dense jungle. The leaves were thick and the cool air wafted across their senses. They kept silent in their search, their heightened senses giving them perfect night vision. They only walked for about five minutes when a deafening roar traveled toward them. Only one creature made a sound like that: the *thanka-ta* beast. The *thanka-ta* beast was one of the most dangerous creatures that stalked the jungle. They only roared like that when they hunted their prey.

He could have pushed it aside, thinking it hunted a smaller jungle creature. He stood there and closed his eyes, focusing his advanced hearing on his surroundings. He could have pushed the roar aside, assuming the beast just hunted, but as he listened, other noises made themselves known. He heard two hearts beating a fast rhythm, the loud thumping of two frightened hearts. He knew those two heart beats were Mena and Kitty, and he knew they were in trouble. About to send his warriors in the direction of the beast, he picked up two swift movements off to the side. He immediately caught sight of Mena's long hair flowing behind her and the light color of Kitty's hair as the two ran quickly.

The heavy thick leaves slapped them on every exposed body part. Demariak didn't wait any longer, just took off through the woods towards the females. He turned his head and saw Keriak run next to him, his expression fierce. Far on the other side, the warriors stealthily moved towards the beast. He saw in horror as the beast closed in on the females, only a few feet away from them.

* * * *

Mena's legs burned from the running. Her lungs strained from the big gulps of air she sucked in. She could feel the monster closing in on them, and she felt hopelessness settle in.

So this is how I die, at the mercy of a horrible beast from my nightmares.

She didn't want to say her thought out loud, didn't want to make Kitty any more scared then she already was, if that were even possible.

She stumbled over her own feet, causing Kitty to stumble as well. They both fell to the ground. Their breathing raged, and their hearts pounded. About to regain her footing, she froze at the feel of warm, moist breath cascading down her back. She looked into Kitty's face to see her friend's eyes wide with fear. Ever so slowly, Mena turned her head and saw a huge, gaping mouth with razor-sharp teeth. Its slime-like drool fell to the ground, the sound of it hitting the dirt making her feel sick.

She didn't need to tell Kitty to run, instinct causing them to move. Through the corner of her eye, she saw Kitty's body momentarily freeze. Gripping her hands in the dirt, she tensed her legs and shot up ready to make a getaway. As Kitty ran only inches ahead of her, Mena chanced a look behind her only to regret the act. The beast closed in, bringing its deadly-sharp tail up like a scorpion about to strike. Looking forward, she felt a cool whoosh of air behind her before she felt a piercing pain strike her in the back. She stumbled again from the impact, forcing herself to block out the pain and continue to run.

* * * *

Demariak watched in horror as the beast cut into Mena. He moved more quickly, shouting out his orders to the warriors just feet from the beast. In unison, they all pulled out their bows, their arrows flying through the air and striking the beast. He was so close to them, yet so far away. He pushed his body harder than ever before, not caring that the branches cut against his flesh.

The beast roared as the arrows pierced its flesh, its tail whipping furiously back and forth. The plan worked, though, and the beast stopped hunting the females, its mouth trying feverishly to rip the arrows from its body. Arrow after arrow flew into its body as Demariak's warriors moved closer to the beast. He was so close, so close to the females that he could hear their heavy panting.

It wasn't just the cut that worried him; it was the poison the beast injected into its prey that was the deadliest. He needed to get to Mena fast before the poison fully circulated in her blood. If it set into her muscles and bones, it would be too late.

He ate up the distance, Keirak right on his heels and going straight for Kitty. The females were slowing, their bodies about to give in to exhaustion. The females stumbled again, and that was when he looped his arm around Mena's waist. She gave a gasp as he scooped her into his arms and picked up his speed.

He pumped his legs harder, his feet taking them farther away from the beast. Keirak's moves were quick and steady behind him, and he chanced a looked behind him. Kitty was draped across his arms, her whole body curled inward. He was aware of the war cries echoing through the trees—his men closing in on the beast. He would have gotten great pleasure from killing the beast himself, but right now, Mena was what mattered.

He didn't know what ruled him more: the anger that he felt that Mena hadn't listened to him, or the fear that she would be taken away from him. Mena wept in his arms, her soft cries making his heart clench.

"Shhh, it's okay, my love. You're safe now!" She sagged in his arms, her crying slowly calming down. He held her tighter, his eyes taking in their surroundings. He could hear nothing advancing on them and knew his men were doing their job.

He could smell the blood from her wound and knew it was deep. The warm stickiness of it coated his arm, running down his hand. He wanted to comfort her but knew it wasn't the time or place for such actions. Running toward a deep gorge in the ground, he slowed and then finally stopped. Keirak stepped next to him, Kitty in his arms, her soft cries audible.

Demariak stared down at Mena, her eyes wide with fear and the moisture from her tears glistening in the moonlight. He knew she couldn't see him as well as he could her, but nonetheless, she reached her hands toward him and whispered his name softly.

"It will be ok, *thalla*. I am going to take you to the healer." He pulled her closer into his body, her small frame starting to shiver uncontrollably. "Keirak, I need you to finish it. I will take the females back to the mountain; Mena needs the healer right away. He turned towards Keirak, who stared at Kitty with longing. He didn't say anything, just dipped his head and kissed Kitty on the head.

He looked at Demariak, nodded his head and gently set Kitty on the ground. He was gone before another word was said, his movements so fast he was nowhere to be seen.

Chapter Seventeen

Keirak hated leaving Kitty but knew there were no other options at the moment. As he swiftly ran toward the other warriors, he could already smell blood, and not just from the beast. He reached a clearing where the men were all standing in a loose circle around the beast.

The *Thanka-ta* beast mostly relied on movement to catch its prey, so they had a big advantage. The creature was fierce, its weaknesses minimal. Because it had such poor eye sight, it relied on transmitting.

As he silently crouched mere feet from the loose circle of warriors, he knew the men could already sense him. At the moment, the beast seemed confused, its head thrashing back and forth, trying to locate them. It could sense them but was disoriented and confused.

Keirak didn't even flinch when the beast let out a horrendous roar, its tail whipping back and forth and its claws outstretched. This was a predictable tactic, a defense mechanism it used to frighten its prey out of hiding. Keirak took the opportunity while the beast was distracted and moved closer to the circle. He signaled for the other warriors to do the same, each one of them silent and precise in their movements. As the warriors quickly made room, the beast froze and whipped its body around until it stared directly at Keirak.

* * * *

Demariak had Mena cradled in one arm and Kitty hanging onto his back. His legs ate up the ground, and within moments he could see the entrance to the cave.

"Is she going to be all right?"

Kitty's soft voice vibrated against his back, and he looked down at Mena. Her eyes were barely open, and her breathing was growing slower by the second. "I hope so."

That was the best answer he could give her, the most honest one. He truly didn't know if she would be all right, and as Kitty wept against his back, he wished he could reassure her more… reassure himself more.

* * * *

As Keirak stared at the *Thanka-ta* beast, he couldn't help the fury that went through him because the females had gotten hurt from this creature. Kitty may not have gotten injured, but he knew she would forever be emotionally scarred. He couldn't even imagine what Demariak was going through right now. All his life he fought the creatures of his planet and had gotten injured in the process. He never, though, in all his time had such an intense desire to slaughter one of the beasts as he did right now.

With Demariak not able to lead, Keirak was put in charge. The warriors waited silently for him to give orders, and he knew he would need their help in defeating the beast. He craved, needed to deliver the first hard blow. Keeping his body still, he brought his arm around slowly to grip the *neeko* whip he had attached to his body. One strike to the beast's body wouldn't bring it down, but it would stun it enough for him and his warriors to make their move.

The beast roared as it caught the slight movement he made and went into a crouching stance. It stayed in that position, momentarily frozen in place as it waited. In a lightning flash of movement, Keirak brought the whip out and into a wide arc. It whistled through the night air, making contact with the beast's back.

The deafening roar would have made a lesser warrior blink, but for him, it only made his irritation spike. Catching a fast movement above, the creature's needle-sharp tail slashed through the air. Throwing himself to the ground and rolling to the side, Keirak barked out an order to the warriors. The sharp, poisonous tip of the tail struck the ground mere inches from his body.

That was all it took for his men to attack the beast with skilled precision. Standing up, he picked up the *neeko* whip, which had fallen to the ground in his quick movements, and whipped it around his head in a circular motion. He twisted it so that it wrapped around the beast's neck. The creature's tail slashed through the night, trying to make contact with anything.

Fury contorted the beast's features as the warriors attacked it. Gripping the whip tighter caused it to tighten around the beast's neck. Popping noises sounded around him as the whip's poison-filled stones broke and penetrated the beast's skin. Its claws slashed out, making contact with a few of the warriors. Its claws didn't carry the same noxious poison as its tail did, but they were sharp and could cut a body in half. It whipped its tail again, slashing across his leathers and forcing him to the ground.

Gripping his arm, the warriors rushed the beast, taking it to the ground quickly. The warriors circled the fallen creature and tightened the leathers that wrapped around its body. With the beast temporarily restrained, a few of the warriors went to the injured males to see to their wounds. The *Thanka-ta* beast flailed around, trying to slash out at the warriors even though it was restrained. Even though the poison in the whips would have paralyzed a smaller creature, it didn't much faze the *Thanka-ta*.

Keirak pulled himself off the ground, thankful the beast had only gotten his leathers. Staring the beast in the eye, Keirak reached behind him and brought out his six-foot sword. Bringing it in front of the beast's eyes, he made sure the creature could see its sharp point. The beast hissed at him, showing its rows and rows of disgusting, serrated teeth. It tried to lunge forward, snapping at him. Just as the beast was about to make contact with him, he brought the sword down, cleanly cutting the head from its body. Even though it was decapitated, it still snapped its jaw open and closed, its body twisting on the ground.

Wiping his sword on his leather-clad thigh, he left the beast on the ground to die.

Chapter Eighteen

Demariak moved quickly through the tunnels of the mountain, pushing past anyone that stood in his way. Kitty tried to keep up with him, her crying echoing off the stone walls.

"Kitty, please go back to your chamber. I will send Keirak for you once I safely get Mena to the healer." She cried harder behind him, and he clenched his jaw. It pained him to hear her cries, but she was a distraction he couldn't afford right now.

Mena's eyes were closed, her breathing almost nonexistent.

"Will you tell me how she is as soon as you get word?"

"Yes, Kitty."

He was thankful when he didn't hear her behind him any longer and breathed out a sigh. He picked up his pace, taking the last turn and seeing the healer's chamber ahead.

* * * *

Kitty paced her room, going back and forth in front of her bed. She chewed on her nails, so nervous she could not stand to be still. Tears streamed down her cheeks at the thought of Mena lying so still in Demariak's arms. She hated herself, wished she was the one who had gotten hurt instead of Mena. If she had just listened to Mena, none of this would have happened. A light knock sounded at her door, and she rushed over to it, praying it was word about Mena. She threw the door open, surprised to see Keirak standing on the other side.

"Is she okay?"

She stuck her head around the door frame, looking both ways before stepping back inside. She knew Keirak couldn't understand her, but the question had been rattling in her head since they had gotten back to the mountain. He stared at her, sadness covering his strong features. She twisted her hands together, her heart beating wildly against her ribs. He took a couple of steps towards her, and she swallowed. Tears continued to stream down her cheek, and she wished he couldn't see her looking so vulnerable.

He passed the threshold, mere feet from her. She felt his body heat radiating off of him. Her emotions were so strong, so fierce that she needed to feel something other than them. She took the few steps that separated them and wrapped her arms around his waist. He tensed against her, but she didn't care. He felt so good against her, his hard body giving her the strength she didn't have. He whispered something against her hair, his hands running slow circles against her back. She cried harder against his chest, thankful for the comfort he gave her.

"Oh Keirak, I hope Mena is okay."

"Detta ka thentta, vu, Keena."

* * * *

Surprise engulfed Keirak when Kitty wrapped her small arms around his waist. Since her arrival to Dimi of the Seven Moons, she had been so distant with him. Although he knew she was probably just emotional over everything that had happened, he welcomed her warm embrace. Even though he would have preferred her embrace to be because she cared for him, he would take what he could get. He couldn't help the endearment that slipped out and was thankful that she didn't understand his native tongue. He knew she didn't realize that when he said "Detta ka thentta, vu, Keena", it meant *"Worry no more, my heart."*

He never felt shame or disappointment for never learning the English tongue, for he never had the opportunity when he was a young child. But now that Kitty had come into his life, he wished he had learned it so he could tell her the endearments in her native English.

He knew when everything passed, she would probably go back to disliking him. He should keep his distance, had heard as much from the other warriors, but he couldn't help himself. He felt possessive and territorial around her, felt himself warm at the sight of her smile when she smelled one of the garden flowers. He knew she always thought no one could see her, and because of that fact, her smile was always genuine. His heart swelled with a feeling he had never felt before.

Looking down at her, he absently rubbed his thumbs over the soft swells of her cheeks. Her beauty astounded him, bewitched him and made his heart stop. But, he knew she would never accept him or a life in his world. He just couldn't bring himself to let her go, though. He knew she wanted desperately to leave, to go back to what she knew. He would give her anything her heart desired, would give her the moons if her heart desired.

She silently cried against him, her small hands gripping his back. He pulled away, gently taking her small hand and leading her out of her chamber. She gave no resistance, just followed him with sadness in her eyes. He didn't know how Mena was, but maybe Demariak could give her some good news about Mena, or at least he hoped he could. She walked by his side, her warm hand still in his. Her sweet scent washed through him, warming his chest. She was his *keena*, his heart. He whispered more endearments and encouragements to her. He told her that everything would be okay, hoping that what he said wasn't in vain.

Chapter Nineteen

Demariak paced in front of the healer's chamber, waiting for word about Mena's condition. She was so close to death by the time he arrived at the healer's chambers. Once he finally reached the healer, he could do nothing but kneel on the ground and let the servants take Mena from his arms. They carried her still form into the sacred chamber, the doors shutting him out and breaking his heart further.

He would have brought her into the chamber himself, but it was forbidden to enter unless one practiced the high healing arts or had been an inducted, loyal servant of the *Chachina,* the high healer. Even Demariak, being the leader of all the ZorZack tribe, followed the same rules as all others. At that moment, though, he wanted to barge through the double doors and take Mena's small hand into his. He wanted to comfort her, make sure she knew how much he cared for her. He didn't, though, and just sat on the cold ground and waited.

He couldn't stop the hollow ache that filled his chest, the emptiness that he felt when they plucked Mena out of his arms. He now sat on a stone bench, the *koola* and *jaggina* flowers' potent scents coating the small waiting area. His senses were numb, and not even the smell of those beautiful healing flowers was able to inspire him.

Keirak had brought Kitty by. Kitty's face was red and wet from her tears. She insisted on staying until they heard word about Mena, but Demariak had talked her into going with Keirak and getting something to eat.

Running a hand over his face, Demariak stared at the floor, moving his foot in a repetitive motion. Elbows on his knees, he placed his face in his hands and breathed a weary sigh. The chamber door finally opened and out stepped the *Chachina,* her face tired from the strain. He stood up instantly and watched as the *Chachina* slowly walked up to him and stared into his eyes. She stood several feet shorter than him, and her age far surpassed his own. Her flowing white hair brushed her hips. Her eyes, the color of the darkest waters, reflected her immense knowledge.

He worriedly looked down at the healer. "Great *Chachina,* please bring good news about my *thalla.*" He didn't care that a warrior such as himself spoke such endearments in front of others. He was their ruler, and his love lay injured in the next room.

The healer stared at him, her knowing eyes so wise. His fear increased at her silence. She held up a slender, wrinkled hand for him to be silent.

"Worry not, great lord, for your queen is well."

Relief washed through him at the knowledge that she would be okay. His body sagged, his big shoulders slumping.

"You are lucky you brought the young female to me when you did." Taking her fragile body over to the stone bench, the healer sat down, making sure all of her *kooka* robes where in their rightful place. "The poison advanced through her system rapidly, and she hallucinated about… a private moment between the two of you."

She cleared her throat, and he knew the healer had heard things she wished she hadn't.

"She is healthy and well, but there have been some things that came up during my healing session that you should be aware of."

A dread settled in Demariak's stomach at that thought that something could be terribly wrong. Would there be an illness that she would carry with her through her life? Would the poison leave lasting effects? How he wanted to rush right in there and cradle her body close to his, feel her warmth settle down to his bones and give him the reassurance that he needed—that he craved. He listened in numb shock at what the healer revealed to him in those next moments.

He made his way toward the healer's chamber door, stopping and looking back at the healer. He turned back to the closed doors, his emotions wild inside of him. He stared at the door for long moments, seeing each grain of the wood swirl together in a hypnotizing collection. He wanted nothing more than to rush back there and hold Mena in his arms. He wanted to bust through the doors, show anyone who watched whom he possessed, what was his to keep safe. He didn't, though, just turned away and headed back to his chamber. Mena still lay unconscious. The healer informed him that she needed all the healing rest she could get. He clenched his jaw, forcing himself to keep moving and not turn back.

* * * *

Two days passed since Demariak had brought Mena to the healer. He felt on edge, his temper flaring at every small thing. Everyone steered clear of him, knowing why he acted the way he did. He paced his chamber, waiting impatiently as the time ticked down until he could see her. She would be transferred today to another chamber now that her strength had grown. He sat down on his bed, his pacing causing tracks in the floor. Just a few moments longer, and he could be with Mena.

He walked briskly toward the chamber Mena now stayed in, his heart pounding so fast he thought it would explode. Stopping at the closed double doors, he took a deep breath and pushed them open. In the center of the room stood a great stone platform topped with pillows, furs, and blankets made from the finest fabrics. The candles burned low, framing the bed and making a soft halo of light around it. Several stone slabs sat around the room, holding various natural elements the *Chachina* used in her healing.

Walking toward the stone platform, he sucked in a breath when he saw how pale Mena was. She looked so frail and fragile, her small body covered in blankets. She breathed heavily, her body in a deep healing sleep. He couldn't stop the joy that rushed through him. To know she was indeed alive and well made him ecstatic.

Closing his eyes, he ran a hand through his short hair, breathing out a deep breath he hadn't realized he held. Almost as if she sensed him, she moved slightly in the bed, her face grimacing in pain. He rushed to her side, his big war-callused hand running over her hair. He whispered softly to her, telling her how precious she was.

"Demariak, is that you?"

Her voice sounded soft, so distant and weak. He clenched his jaw and closed his eyes, joy radiating through him at her state of well-being. "Shh, it's okay, *thalla*. I'm here now, and everything will be okay." He kissed her lightly on the forehead. Her eyes opened and looked up into his face.

"What happened? I mean, I remember the creature, and you and Keirak rescuing us, but after that it becomes a blur. And then, it just goes black." She turned to her side, moaning lightly.

Demariak caressed her shoulders, stopping her movements. He stared at her, knowing worry covered his face. He held her hands, bringing them to his mouth and gently kissing them.

"I'm fine, really. Just a little sore, that's all." She smiled at him, thankful when he visibly relaxed. "Oh, my gosh. Kitty. Where's Kitty? Is she all right?" Panic threaded through her voice, and he ran his hand along her cheek, willing her to be calm.

"Please be calm, *thalla*, so you don't injure your healing back. Kitty is fine and uninjured." He smiled down at her, running his hand lightly down her cheek. "I thought I lost you, *thalla*." Breathing out heavily, he took her hands into his and brought them to his mouth for another soft kiss. "I don't know what I would have done if you had left me. My life would have been over, *thalla*." Moving in, he lightly kissed her on the lips and rested his forehead against hers.

* * * *

She breathed a sigh of contentment at being in Demariak's arms. His hand rubbed lightly over her stomach, the caress soft and caring. She frowned and looked down at his hand. Confusion laced her senses as she looked back at his face. They stared at each other, Demariak gently pulling her into a soft embrace. He seemed careful of her still-healing wound as he pulled her against his chest.

He gently laid her back on the bed, his hand smoothing over her hair. His big palm went back to her stomach, the warmth of it spearing the loose gown she wore. "Demariak, what's going on?"

"The *Chachina* spoke with me when she finished healing you."

"The what?" She tried to pull back and look at him, but he kept a soft yet firm hold on her.

"Please, my love, be still. There's nothing for you to be worried about."

He breathed in deeply, his eyes closing momentarily.

"The *Chachina* is what we call our great healer, *thalla*. She healed you when I thought I had lost you. We spoke, and she has come across something that we didn't think could happen."

Her forehead furrowed, not really understanding what he meant. His palm once again rubbed her belly in soft rhythmic movements. Her breath hitched as everything finally dawned on her.

She shook her head and looked down at his hand on her belly. "Are you saying what I think you're saying?" She looked into his eyes, her mouth slightly ajar. "Are you saying that I'm... pregnant?" She laughed, the sound soft and amazed. He looked down at her in confusion, which only seemed to increase her laughter.

"Is this the response females in your dimension have when they find out such a thing?" He was completely confused. This was a reaction he hadn't expected.

She reached up and ran her hand across his face. "No, it's not the traditional response. I'm laughing because it shocked me... and I'm happy." He smiled at her, a long breath escaping him.

"The *Chachina* told me it came to her attention while she healed you that you were with young. *Thalla*, you carry my young within you." He lowered himself and laid a soft kiss against her belly. He whispered words in his language, lifting up and taking her mouth in a gentle kiss.

He knew she didn't understand his language but knew the words he spoke were meant to soothe, to comfort. The knowledge that she would be the mother of his child bounced around in his head, amazing him further. She put her hand over his, opening her mouth and accepting his tongue. Their mouths fused together, their tongues running over each other in a slow dance.

He broke the kiss, smiling down at her. "We're going to be parents." She smiled up at him. She laughed again, rising up and initiating the next kiss. He didn't miss the mask of pain that momentarily crossed her features. He gently but forcefully pushed her back down, covering her stomach with his palm again. "You must be still, your body still hasn't fully healed." He leaned down and kissed her softly. "My sweet, sweet Mena, you are to be my queen and the mother of my young. There is nothing in this world or any other that could make me any more pleased." He kissed her on the top of her head and pulled away. "You need to rest, my love. I will be back later with something for you to eat." He kissed her one last time before leaving.

* * * *

Mena lay there, her mind running through her new knowledge. She couldn't wait to tell Kitty. She couldn't have asked for anything better than to have Demariak be the father of her child. It made the small miracle growing inside of her that much more special.

He returned later that night, carrying a tray of food. He fed her by hand, making sure she finished every piece of food he brought. Demariak explained the pregnancies of the *ZorZack* females to Mena even though they didn't know if hers would be the same. She was shocked to hear that the gestation period was only four months in their world. There had never been a human pregnant from a *ZorZack* warrior before, so they were both going into this blind.

That night they did nothing but hold each other, whispering soft, loving words to one another. They lay like that for hours, finally falling asleep wrapped in each other's embrace.

Epilogue

Four months later

"Mmm, that feels so good." Rolling onto her back, Mena looked into a set of ice-blue eyes that were heavy-lidded and filled with deep lust. Spreading her legs wider, she closed her eyes and moaned softly at the feel of Demariak's hand running up and down her swollen, wet pussy lips. His mouth roamed down her neck, gently biting and then laving the pleasure-pain away with his tongue.

She arched her back, thrusting her breast out for his touch. The warm, wet swipe of his tongue against her already-stiff nipples caused goose bumps to pop out on her skin. Spearing her hands through his short, silky hair, she pushed her breasts farther into his mouth, wringing a moan from him. She gasped when his teeth rasped over her elongated nipple. His hand moved lower, his thumb running over her swollen clit.

Spreading her legs wide, she thrust her hips up, needing his fingers—among other things—deep inside of her.

She watched as he kissed each breast, slowly moving lower down her body with his mouth. He left a path of wet kisses and small bites along her exposed skin, inflaming her senses higher. Her breathing picked up as he neared her wet pussy. He looked up before he kissed her pussy lips. She closed her eyes, moaning his name, and thrust her hips up, begging him without words.

He smiled up at her, flicking her clit with his thumb and running his other finger along the opening of her pussy. His mouth covered her clit, plucking at it wildly. He lifted her legs over his shoulders, his big shoulders taking up her entire view. He groaned loudly, his mouth working quickly on her clit. She couldn't help the whimpers that came out of her as her body started to light up.

"Oh please, Demariak, do something, anything."

She brought her hands to her breasts, plucking at her nipples, which grew stiff and long with her arousal. He looked up at her again, his eyes closed partly, arousal covering his face. Her pussy juices coated his fingers, dripping down her leg and onto the bed. The feeling turned her on, making her moan louder.

"Who does this pussy belong to, *thalla*?" He brought his mouth down to her clit and sucked it into his mouth, making her groan and moan. "Who, *thalla*?" There was a fierce possessiveness that came through his voice, a sound that made her arousal grow.

"Oh God, you, Demariak. My pussy belongs to you!"

He growled against her clit, bringing her closer to the edge.

"Fill me. Do it now. Oh, God!" She moaned as his thick finger slid into her channel, his mouth working feverously at her clit. The sucking and the thrusting was all she needed. Her orgasm consumed her, finally bursting through her body and making everything go white with pleasure. Vaguely aware of her surroundings, she heard the animalistic growls coming from Demariak as he continued to wring her orgasm out of her.

Before the pleasure subsided, his big body moved on top of her, the hot hard tip of his erection pressing against her opening. In one thrust, he seated himself fully into her, causing another earth-shattering orgasm to wash through her.

The pleasure was never ending as he thrust in and out of her. She gripped him continuously, her orgasm peaking over and over again. He braced his elbows on either side of her head and pistoned his hips faster. She loved the feel of his balls slapping against her wet skin.

She watched in awe as he threw his head back and roared out his release. The hot jets of his semen poured into her, causing another orgasm to crest within her.

Moments ticked by as they both lay there in blissful exhaustion, their bodies still intimately connected, her inner muscles tightening around his shaft.

* * * *

They lay there, Mena wrapped in his arms, as the two of them breathed heavily.

"You're going to be the death of me, *thalla*." He kissed her on the top of her head while bringing her more tightly against his chest. She softly chuckled, her hand smoothing over his bicep. He propped himself on one elbow and looked down at her with an arched brow. "What's so funny?"

She lightly smacked him on the arm, her smile lighting up the entire room.

"You and your after-sex comments." She gave him a light kiss on the lips and got up at the sound of a light tap on their chamber door. She quickly pulled on her black silk robe and went over to the door. She heard the rustle of sheets and turned to see Demariak pulling the covers over himself. Mena opened the door, and Kitty stood on the other side, her hand raised to knock again.

Kitty adapted well over the course of the past few months, actually becoming closer to Keirak and letting him teach her about their culture. They spent a lot of time together, he teaching her the *ZorZack* language, she teaching him English. Keirak still constantly followed her around like a lost puppy. Although Kitty would look over her shoulder at Keirak and sigh loudly, Mena thought she secretly liked it.

Every chance Kitty got, she apologized for what had happened. Mena couldn't fault Kitty for her near-death experience. It had been her choice to follow in the first place. She was just glad everyone turned out safe and healthy in the end. Kitty even gave up on her crazy escape plans, for the time being anyway.

"I wasn't going to interrupt the two of you, what with all the noise you guys have been making in here, but this little one kept fussing for her momma."

Blushing at Kitty's comment, Mena smiled and looked down at the small bundle she carried. Kitty chuckled as she handed the small bundle over.

Now, as she looked down into the sweet face of her daughter, she felt joy and love at the creation she had made with Demariak. The tiny little girl had her father's ice-blue eyes, and a head full of black springy curls. She said bye to Kitty, and closed the door. She walked over to Demariak, a grin covering his masculine features. She curled up next to him on the bed, tucking the little girl between them. Their daughter, whom they had named *Nea*, meaning hope in Demariak's language, cooed and held her small hands out to her father.

He scooped the little baby up into his arms, giving her a gentle kiss on her tiny forehead, and whispered *I love you*.

Mena couldn't believe how things had turned out. She sighed in contentment, the love she felt swelling hr chest and making her feel so thankful. Mena watched with a smile as *Nea* took hold of Demariak's finger, her grip strong and promising. Mena laid her head against his chest, absorbing his body heat and feeling contentment.

"I love you, Demariak."

"I love you too, *thalla*."

She looked up at him, giving him all of her love, knowing he felt the same way for her. Together they had created a beautiful daughter, a little piece of both of them that would forever keep them connected.

THE END

SIREN PUBLISHING *Classic*

TEMPTATION UNVEILED
Dimi of the Seven Moons

Jenika Snow

TEMPTATION UNVEILED

Dimi of the Seven Moons 2

JENIKA SNOW
Copyright © 2010

Preface

It is a world unlike ours but similar in so many ways. It is a different dimension between our world and the world known as Dimi of the Seven Moons.

They are known as the ZorZacks, a tribe of giant warriors that are led by their king, Demariak and his queen Mena. With insatiable appetites for hunting and passion, they are not to be challenged. Once they claim what's theirs, there is nothing that can take it away. Be prepared to be claimed, possessed, and know unspeakable passion, because once they have what they seek, they will never let it go.

This is their world, their rules.

Prologue

The sun beat down through the trees, making everything the rays touched warm. Sweat soaked him like a second skin, a glistening sheen that shone under the hot sun. Keirak kept his eyes down as he sharpened his blade with a large stone. He wiped his brow with his forearm and glanced up at the busy village before him. The villagers of *KayKow*, his home, went through their daily activities, not missing a beat. The females carried intricately woven baskets on their sides, laughing and talking amongst themselves. The males stuck together in tight-knit groups talking about past hunting stories and superior kills they made throughout their lives.

Being but thirteen, Keirak was still considered a child amongst his tribe, but that didn't stop him from practicing his fighting and stances in the jungle. Sometimes, he talked one of the other boys into fighting against him, but mainly, he fought with the trees. Their bark making perfect targets in which he could train. He dreamed of becoming a great warrior, claiming his prized female, and being able to fight with the other fierce *KayKow* males. He would be a male of worth, a male his mother could be proud of.

His father died a brave warrior when he was a small child, but still, he would make his father proud as well. He cleared his head of idle thoughts and brought his eyes back down to the blade that shined with sharpness. He prepared it for his mother, making it sharp enough for her to cut through any beasts' hide like she was cutting through water.

"What have you there, my son?"

He looked up and shielded his eyes from the blinding light of the sun. His mother stepped to the side, blocking the sun with her body and smiling down at him. Her hair was pulled up, making a few of her blondish gray curls cascade down around her face. Her eyes sparkled with motherly love as she continued to smile at him. "I am sharpening this blade for you, Mother. It will have the sharpest blade in all of the *KayKow* tribe." He stood, his body towering over his petite mother. He wiped the blade on his hide encased thigh and handed it to her.

"Why, my son, you please me to no end. How did I end up with such a loving boy?" She ran her palm down his cheek and took the offered blade. "You are right, this is a marvelous blade." She put the blade in her basket and whispered, "I don't doubt this is the grandest blade in all of the tribe, everyone will be most jealous of me." She kissed him on the cheek and walked away to join the other females.

Everything suddenly became eerily silent, his tribe members becoming still as statues. The wind ceased its movement through the trees, and the wildlife of the jungle seemed to stand still. Giant males swarmed out of every inch of the jungle, their war cries reaching his ears as they held their swords high. He watched, not knowing what to do as *KayKow* warriors rushed females and young out of the way. Intruders started slashing everything and anything they could reach.

Eyes wide, Keirak wanted to rush out and fight like a male of worth, but he was frozen in place, not able to do anything other than watch like a coward. The intruders' swords went through the bodies of the males he had grown up with…his brethren. He watched in horror as they fell, their life source seeping from their bodies and coating the ground. The females' screams pierced every inch of the village, and the *KayKow* warriors war cries boomed through the air. His brethren were a fierce bunch, but too many invaders continued to come out of the jungle. The rogues snatched females off the ground and threw them over their beefy shoulders, their lust clearly reflected in their faces as they fondled the terrified women.

Snapping out of his daze, Keirak looked frantically around for his mother. He spotted her with group of females and was about to sprint toward her when a hand gripped his shoulder and spun him around forcefully. The man in front of him stared down at him with the blackest, coldest eyes Keirak had ever seen. Scars riddled the strangers face, and he wore a hard smirk. He spoke, but Keirak didn't understand the language.

Female cries sounded behind him, but he could do no more than stand there immobilized with fear. The stranger grinned and turned him around so he watched in horror at the circle of females that sobbed, his mother lying on the ground in front of them. He couldn't hold back the roar that broke through his throat. "Mother!" Hot tears slipped down his cheeks, but he didn't try to stop them. His mother lay on the floor, her crumbled body bloody. He had never wept before, but today, for the first time in his life, he cried because his mother lay dead on the filthy ground. The strangers took the younger females and extinguished the older ones, the ones they deemed worthless.

He tore his eyes from his mother's body, that image bound to give him nightmares for the rest of his life. Blood coated everything, so much that it created a thick pool on the dirt ground. Bodies were scattered everywhere, people he grew up with, people he loved. Baskets with fruit were strewn on the ground, their contents spilled over and crushed in the stampede of fighting. He was turned around but didn't bother looking into the scarred strangers face, didn't bother to stop himself from weeping like a child instead of the warrior he wanted to be for his mother.

"You understand me?"

The stranger spoke in the language of Keirak's tribe with a voice so cruel and heartless it sent chills down his spine. Keirak nodded his head and looked into the soulless black eyes of his mother's murderer. The scarred one may not have done the actual slaying, but he was the leader and therefore the killer in Keirak's eyes. The scarred one shrugged his bulky shoulders and smiled.

"Everyone you know is dead now. I should kill you, too, but I think it will be more painful if I spare your worthless hide. Remember my face young one and forever know the pain I have inflicted upon you and yours." He turned and laughed, and all of his men joined in as their leader spoke the cruel and heartless words.

Keirak felt anger and fury build inside of him until it soon consumed his very being. His fear and sadness were pushed to the side, the burning inside of him reaching a boiling point and threatening to explode. With all of his might, he lifted his arm and swung at the demon before him. Before his fist made contact, he was shoved to the ground so hard he felt his breath leave him in a whoosh. He lay on his belly in the dirt, his breath causing the dust to puff around him in clouds. All around him, the deep laughs of the demon men rang through his ears.

"Not big enough nor strong enough to even save your own people, yet you think to strike me?"

More booming laughter sounded behind him as he was kicked in the ribs, the pain shooting through him like knives. As much as his damaged ribs hurt, it didn't compare to the pain he felt in his chest—in his heart. He watched from the ground, not able to move as the demon men looted his village and took the young females. They disappeared into the forest without even a backward glance. He stayed on the ground for hours, his soul and body broken…the only remaining member of the *KayKow* tribe.

Chapter One

Dimi of the Seven Moons, present day

Sitting up in bed, Keirak pressed a hand to his thundering heart and tried to slow his ragged breathing. He often woke like this, sweat dripping from his body, fear and anger coursing through him. He dreamed of his past, relived the nightmare haunting him since he was a boy. He breathed out deeply and ran a hand through his hair, mussing the short locks up even more. Throwing the beast hide off, he padded naked over to the natural waterfall, which served as his bathing chamber.

The alcove held a small, ten foot tall natural heated waterfall and was always the first place he went when he woke from the nightmare. He stepped under the warm water and placed both palms on the smoothed stone. He hung his head and closed his eyes as the hot water cascaded across his skin. He tried to push away the anger and fear that still coursed through him. There was only one thing, only one person that calmed him completely with just a thought…Kitty.

* * * *

Lying in a bed topped with fluffy silken pillows and soft animal hides, Kitty stared at the intricately carved ceiling. It had been a year since she and Mena arrived on this world called *Dimi of the Seven Moons*. She could still remember the day they found the strange portal in their backyard and ended up going through it, only to find themselves in another dimension. After being caught by huge muscled men and taken to their home inside a mountain, they found out how much their lives were about to change.

The world she now lived on was a different dimension on Earth, a world so different and primitive, it was like she traveled back in time. It had taken her a long time to accept that this was her new home. The men were giant warriors who were double her size and always seemed to have fierce expression on their faces. Every time she thought about the mess she dragged Mena into, grief consumed her.

At first, she was bombarded with many emotions from anger, to fear, to frustration, to grief, but in the end, she had come to grips with her situation. It wasn't easy, but what choice did she have?

She still remembered in vivid detail the time she tried to escape. Mena had almost died, something Kitty would have to live with for the rest of her life. She would never attempt anything like that again.

She sat up in bed and looked around her chamber, as everyone in this world called it. It would never look like her old room, with the matching star bedspread and curtains that opened to look out over their small neighborhood. She had gotten used to it though. She missed her computer and phone, even Jell-O and french fries, all the things she used to take for granted, the everyday little things. The walls were bare of materialistic decorations. The only thing covering them was the intricate design carved on every single wall in the mountain fortress.

A light knock sounded on the door and she smiled. "Come in." The door opened and Mena walked in, the little girl on her hip smiling and cooing.

"Hi." Mena said as she set the little girl on the floor. Kitty smiled as Nea waddled over to her. Kitty scooped up the little girl and kissed her on the head.

"Well, hello, my sweet." Kitty looked over at Mena who stood by the door, one hand on her swollen belly.

Mena had ended up falling in love with the ZorZack tribe leader and King, Demariak. After Mena had almost lost her life, she found out she carried his child and that ZorZack pregnancies were very different from the ones on Earth. It was hard for her and Mena to grasp that fact, but as her belly grew bigger and faster than it should have for the pregnancies they were used to, they became fast believers. So, after a few months, Mena had given birth to their daughter, Nea, and was pregnant again.

Nea squirmed on her lap, wanting to get to the ground so she could find something to get into. Kitty set her on the ground, her black ringlets bouncing as she crawled around the room. "Sit down. Your feet must be killing you."

"Uh, you have no idea. She runs me ragged, and it doesn't help that I'm carrying around this watermelon." Mena sat on the bed and let herself fall back, letting out a blissful sigh.

She was due to have her and Demariak's second child in a month, and looked every bit of it. She came by everyday, and Kitty suspected it was because Mena worried about her. She would have every right to be in the beginning, but now things were different. Kitty accepted this place as her home because, frankly, what other option did she have? She wasn't about to leave her best friend or the child she loved, and well, there was one other thing that made her want to stay…Keirak. She didn't like to think about how he had somehow wormed his way into her heart, and she really didn't want to look too deeply into the feelings he stirred within her.

They spoke about what was new in the tribe, and Kitty let herself smile as she listened to the stories about the men and women she now called friends.

"So, how are things going with you?"

Kitty hesitated for a second, and Mena's face became a mask of worry. She pulled herself up and stared at Kitty, concern etched all over her face. Kitty held up a hand, stopping any and all questions that were about to come from Mena. "I'm fine. You ask me that every time I see you, but really, I should be asking you that question." The memories of Mena lying in Demariak's arms came crashing back, guilt curling itself around Kitty's heart. She told Mena she was fine, but in all reality, she felt overwhelming guilt for putting Mena in danger.

"Did I ever tell you what a bad liar you are? Why can't you talk to me? We used to talk all the time."

Kitty looked down at their conjoined hands and then back at Mena. She hated lying to her best friend, but she didn't want to talk about the past. She already thought about that horrible night everyday, talking about it would just make it worse. She was just about to brush Mena's question away when she saw the deep sorrow on her friend's soft features. "Hey, what's wrong with you?"

"I just wish you would open up to me, tell me what you're thinking."

"I just don't like to talk about it."

"About what?"

"You know what I'm talking about." She saw confusion on Mena's face before it turned into a scowl.

"I thought we talked about this Kitty. Why do you beat yourself up about what happened?"

"Because! It was my fault that you almost died."

"How can it be your fault when I chose to go with you?"

Mena's warm hand rested atop hers, all of her love and friendship pouring through that slight touch but doing nothing to wash away the guilt that Kitty still harbored. "My guilt over what happened will never go away, ever. If it was the other way around, would you not feel responsible?" Mena cast her eyes down, not voicing her answer to the question. "That's what I thought."

"Listen, you're right. I would feel awful, but it's been a year, Kitty. I didn't die, and it wasn't your fault. I hate to see you suffering. It breaks my heart." Mena stood and picked up Nea, sitting back down on the bed and holding the baby in her lap. "Can we just forget about what happened and start living for today? We can't change the past, so what's the point of dwelling on it?"

Kitty smiled, but it was just for show. She would never be able to forget about it or move on. It wasn't just because it had happened to Mena, although that made it all that worse. If she had put anyone's life in danger she would have felt the same. Kitty kept her smile plastered on, thankful when a knock sounded at the door, the previous conversation temporarily forgotten as Mena set Nea on the ground and got up to answer it.

"It's just Demariak. He wants to have a romantic dinner before he goes out hunting." As soon as Mena opened the door, Demariak wrapped her in a powerful embrace. "*Valla,* how I've missed you. Hello, Kitty."

She gave a little wave before turning her head as the two of them became caught up in an intimate embrace. She got off the bed and picked up Nea, who managed to find a drawer to get into. As soon as the baby saw her father, she cooed and held her chubby, little hands out to him.

Saying goodbye to the trio, Kitty lay back on her bed, feeling lonelier than she had ever felt. Kitty got up, quickly undressing and made her way to the waterfall alcove. She wanted to wash up before heading to the garden chamber to meet with Keirak for their daily language lesson. Since being with the ZorZack tribe, she had spent a lot of time with Keirak.

She was thankful her hands didn't shake anymore every time she felt or saw something that reminded her of home, or smelled something that sparked a memory of her former life. It was the little things that she missed—the food, her vanilla scented shampoo, even her simple flannel pajamas. She had changed since the beginning, but whether that was for the good or the bad, she still didn't quite know. It was hard at first, trying to get comfortable with everything and everyone. She felt safe with Keirak, felt safe knowing he offered her his strong and silent support.

She shook her head of her absent-minded thoughts and finished washing up. She slipped on one of her gowns—a *non-transparent* gown. She refused to wear the transparent dresses the women of the tribe wore, and when Keirak found out, his face had broken into a full grin. She remembered that day so clearly it still surprised her.

She had wrapped an animal hide around her as she kicked the pile of transparent dresses toward Keirak. She had screamed and yelled at him, knowing he couldn't understand her but not giving a damn. She admitted to acting like a child, stomping her foot and breathing out her nose, but she was so furious. He stared at her for a suspended moment, looking between her and the pile of material at his feet before his lips slowly lifted up. That just pissed her off. She cursed him out of her room, surprised when he actually listened. The next day he had stopped by her room and handed her a box full of dresses—non-transparent dress to be precise. After that, she and Keirak spent every day together. She started teaching him English, and he started teaching her the ZorZack language.

She looked at herself in the polished metal hanging by the waterfall that served as a mirror. The majority of the dresses Keirak gave her were shades of blue, and she had wondered if it had anything to do with her eye color. She stepped out of her room and headed toward the garden where she and Keirak always did their language lessons. Her heart pounded the same frantic beat it always did when she was going to meet him.

She walked through the stone hallways, her blurry reflection walking next to her on the polished walls. She turned the corner and made her way toward the entrance of the garden, her favorite place in the whole mountain. Her heart pounded hard against her ribs in anticipation. Her hand landed on the door, and she gently pushed it open, the soft glow of the candles washing over her.

She stood in the opening and looked at Keirak's huge, muscled body hunched over a piece of paper. She walked in and gently shut the door behind her, the wood making a soft click as it closed. His head snapped up, and their eyes met and held. She swallowed at his intense green stare and walked toward him. "Hello Keirak." Before she could pull the seat out to sit down, he had it pulled out for her. "Thank you." She stared at him, her feelings growing for him each and every day. It scared her a little, feeling the things she felt when she really didn't want to. It was easier for her to pretend in this world, to not get connected with people who would only make it seem final.

"You are welcome. How are you?"

His English was very good, so good that it amazed her that he had picked up on it so fast. His accent was deep and thick, which made her tingle in all the right places. Kitty on the other hand had a much harder time with his language, and could only say the bare minimum. "Fine, thank you. What are you reading?" She craned her neck at the thick parchment paper in front of him, and her breath caught. He slid the paper across the table to her. She sat back in her seat, staring with wide eyes at was in front of her.

She ran her fingers over the picture, a drawing so lifelike it looked like a photo. Everything was drawn in black except for her eyes, which were colored bright blue. In the picture, she had a small smile on her lips and looked off to the side. She looked at Keirak. He stared at her so intently she became a little unnerved. "Did you draw this?" The words came out on a breath, the last one catching as she watched him.

"You don't like it?"

She swallowed and looked down at the picture again, running her fingers across the textured paper. "I love it." She whispered the words and glanced up at him.

"I couldn't get you out of my mind, so the other night, I drew it."

She cleared her throat. "Thank you. It's beautiful, but I can't accept it." She didn't want to feel the things she felt, the strong emotions that coursed through her.

"Why not?" His voice hardened slightly, and she worried she had offended him.

"Because, if I accept this, it would mean everything is final." If she let herself feel something for Keirak, then it would be over, her future here would be sealed, and she didn't know if she could accept that. She might be accustomed to living here, but the idea of permanency seemed too hard to grasp. She set the drawing aside and smiled at him. "So, where did we leave off?" His lime green gaze stayed on her for a while before he nodded and looked down.

"I was teaching you common phrases used by the tribe." He slid a thick piece of parchment across the table.

She turned it around and stared at the unusual symbols and letters that she had become familiar with. "Why am I having such a hard time learning this and you already speak English fluently?"

He shrugged. "My tribe was good with languages." He turned his head to the side, his jaw clenching as if he hadn't meant to say what he just said.

"You mean the ZorZack tribe?"

He stayed quiet, his head still cast to the side. "No."

She sat back in her seat and stared at him in confusion. "What do you mean?" He sighed and leaned back against his seat, his eyes capturing hers and holding them. Over the past year, they really hadn't spoken about personal issues.

"Before I joined the ZorZacks, my native tribe was called the *KayKows*. We lived over the *Boccie* Mountains and across the *Zella* Sea."

"Was?" His body tensed slightly, and she immediately regretted asking him.

"My native tribe is no more. Another tribe ambushed us and slaughtered the males and elderly females before taking the younger females with them."

She gasped and covered her mouth with her hand, fighting back tears of sorrow that threatened to spill. "I-I'm so terribly sorry." The fact that he had went through something so horrifying broke her heart, but the fact that he shared it with her warmed her with gratitude. She reached across the table and placed her hand on top of his much larger one. He stiffened at her touch, and she instantly withdrew her hand, wondering if her actions had offended him. "I'm sorry." The fact that he seemed to not like her touch felt like a kick in the gut. His jaw was clenched as he watched her, pierced her with his gaze that seemed electrified and heated. It made her positively shiver with awareness.

Chapter Two

Keirak's body stiffened as Kitty's warm hand settle atop his. His heart pounded fiercely in his chest, and his blood heated under his skin. Her touch felt so right, so good, that he knew he would never get enough of it. Her hand was gone as quickly as it had arrived and he instantly missed her warmth. Ever since he'd laid eyes on her, he couldn't get her out of his mind. He pictured them together, limbs moving as one as he pushed into her soft body and brought them both a pleasure he knew would be incredible.

Since she had arrived a year ago, he hadn't been able to relieve himself with another female. Just thinking about it made his cock go flaccid with distaste. It confused him at first, not knowing how to feel about the emotions she conjured inside of him. Every minute he was near her made him care about her that much more, made his need to protect and cherish her that much more intense

He knew he had to have her, that no other would do. As he stared at her beautiful, soft face, he pictured them together, their life as one and the children they would have. He knew he didn't just want her to sate his lust. No, he wanted her for the rest of his life. His hands shook to touch her, to run his finger along her soft face, smooth away the frown that seemed to mar her beautiful features regularly.

He shouldn't have the thoughts that he had, but they were unavoidable. Females like Kitty needed a gentle male, not one that killed without remorse, not one that had a past that haunted them and woke them with nightmares.

Until she came along, he didn't have any emotions. He was an empty shell of a male that found a quick release with a willing female.

Scars riddled him physically as well as emotionally. He wanted her with a passion he had never felt before, but he knew he had nothing to give her except a haunted past.

He watched as her lovely golden hair fell across her shoulder, her delicate fingers brushing the silken strands back to reveal her slender, creamy neck. He could just picture those golden strands brushing across her breasts and flowing over her nipples that would be hard from his mouth. His cock swelled beneath his leathers, and he shifted uncomfortably in his seat. He felt like a vile monster for thinking such thoughts about her, but he couldn't seem to help himself.

He shouldn't have even given her the picture, but he wanted to give her something that showed his affection, even if it was a small slip of paper. An impulse had urged him to present it to her as an offering, a gift of his affection. He ran his eyes over her body, the image enough to fuel his desires. She wore one of the dresses he brought her, the fabric fitting her body like a second skin and molding to her assets perfectly. He had been elated when she refused to wear the traditional dresses the ZorZack females wore. Truth be told, he would have preferred her to be covered from head to toe in a *Kalla* monster hide.

Before she came along, he preferred his females naked and spread before him, but now things were much different. He wanted to be sweet with her, wanted to be *different* for her. His eyes went down to her supple breasts, two perfect round globes that pressed against her gown. He picked out the dresses from one of the many merchants within the tribes mountain village, choosing the blue hues that matched her eyes.

"So, where should we start?"

He snapped his eyes up, his mind immediately thinking of illicit things of *where* they could start. He pictured her on her belly, her ass up in the air, her pussy wet and waiting for his cock. He shook his head, his leathers starting to grow tighter at the image of her spread out for him. He was thankful her attention was on the parchment with his tribe's language on it, her eyebrows knitted together in confusion.

He cleared his throat and looked at the parchment, thankful he wouldn't have to rise and show his desire that was hard and clearly evident. "These are the most common phrases. I thought we would go over them again since you seemed to have a hard time with them the last time." The most gorgeous shade of pink started to cover her cheeks. Her head went down and he assumed she was ashamed of the fact that she had a hard time with the tribe's language. "Kitty." He reached across the table and placed his finger under her small chin. He lifted her head and their eyes locked. "Do not worry. This language is far from what you are used to. It will take time to learn, but you will catch on, of that I have no doubt."

She didn't say anything, but the way her eyes held his made his cock harder. He hurriedly sat back, brought the parchment closer to him and turned it at an angle. He started at the top and spoke each phrase slowly and clearly. "Tu ma kallena vanya." He looked at her and smiled. "Do you remember what this one means?" She looked at the parchment and knitted her eyebrows together again in thought. He wanted to run his fingers over her brow and smooth away the worry, but he gritted his teeth against the need. Her eyes snapped to his and lit up as a smile crossed her face.

"How are you today?"

"Very good, *fallina*." He immediately closed his mouth and regretted what he just said, hoping she didn't question the phrase he just used. "What about this one?" He quickly pointed to the next phrase, changing the subject and hoping she would notice. Thankfully, she either didn't hear what he said or didn't care. He was relieved she hadn't caught his slip and was annoyed with himself for being so careless.

"Matahka linnatu vunnati." She rubbed her forehead and leaned back against her seat. "I always seem to have trouble with this one. Oh, who am I kidding, I have trouble with all of them." He chuckled lightly, knowing the situation wasn't funny, but not able to help himself.

* * * *

Kitty left the garden room after going over the phrases for two hours. She had a headache from all the concentration, and as much as she wanted to learn the language, she needed a break. She walked slowly back to her room, the same way each and every day. The walls of her new home were so familiar to her, yet so foreign in the same sense. She could see Mena and Nea standing by her bedroom door before she even reached it. "Why are you waiting out here? You know you can just walk in." She scooped up Nea and gave the squirming baby a kiss on the cheek. "Hello sweetie, can you say 'Hi auntie Kitty?'" The little girl squealed and wrapped her chubby, little arms around Kitty before giving her a wet kiss on the chin.

"We just got here and when you didn't answer I assumed you weren't there or that you might be…busy."

Kitty rolled her eyes and opened the door. She walked over to the bed and set the little girl on top of it. "You've got to be kidding."

"Well, it's just that I've noticed how much time you and Keirak are spending with each other, and well, I thought maybe there might be sparks flying."

"Um, that's a no. Keirak and I are just helping each other. I teach him English, and he teaches me the ZorZack language. Although, I have to say I'm really not teaching him anything. The man has picked up on English quicker then I have ever seen." She was not about to tell Mena the feelings that blossomed inside of her for Keirak. That would just end up in a whole lot of speculation, and she didn't want to deal with that. She turned her head and focused her gaze on something else, clasping her hands together as they began to shake.

"Really? Huh. Well, maybe he's just one of those people that can speak five different languages."

"Maybe." She mumbled the word absently and looked down at Nea, who was making herself comfortable on the silk pillows. The little girl brought her thumb into her mouth and started sucking as her eyes started to close.

"Oh, thank goodness. She has been a little hellion today. She even threw food all over the floor. She needs a nice, long nap."

Kitty smiled and ran her fingers through Nea's black ringlets. "So what brings you by, again?"

"I wondered if you wanted to help make journey bags with me and the other women. I meant to ask you when I was by earlier, but it slipped my mind"

"Journey bags?"

"Demariak told me he and some of the other warriors are going out to hunt for food and other supplies. I guess the women make these journey bags that have all sorts of necessities in them."

"Oh. Who's going?"

"Well, Demariak for sure, Draydon, Icezak, and Keirak. I'm not sure if there are more going or not. Demariak said they are long overdue for a trip, and the food is dwindling pretty fast."

She made sure not to let her disappointment show at the thought of Keirak leaving for who knew how long. "Oh, Keirak's going? I wonder why he didn't tell me."

"Demariak just decided on the mission today and hasn't gotten around to telling everyone. He plans on having a meeting later on tonight. Why do you care?" Mena's face broke into a knowing smile. "I knew it! You like him, don't you?"

"Don't be ridiculous, I'm just wondering. Who am I supposed to practice the language with?"

"I'm sure there are plenty of other warriors or even females in the tribe who would help you."

"I don't think so. Keirak and I have this…understanding. It would be weird to start all over with someone else."

"If you say so." Mena looked at her with a skeptical eye and walked over to Nea. She scooped the sleeping baby into her arms and gave her a soft kiss on the forehead.

"When are they making these bag things anyway?"

"Tonight after supper. You don't have to help if you don't want to."

Kitty nodded and watched as Mena adjusted the little girl so she fit comfortably around her swollen belly.

"I just wanted to pass the word along. I'm going to take off and put Nea to bed. If you decide you want to help out, let me know."

She sat on her bed and watched Mena leave, the door shutting without a sound. She stared at the closed door. She reached under the hem of her dress and pulled out the rolled parchment she had hidden there. She unrolled it out on the bed and stared at the drawing of herself. She had told Keirak she couldn't accept it, but how could she *not* accept something Keirak had given her? She had grabbed it when they were leaving, when his back was to her. She was letting her emotions get the better of her. As much as she wanted to keep her distance, it was getting harder and harder. She rolled the parchment up and placed it under her pillow. She lay down on the bed and stared up at the ceiling, her thoughts instantly going to Keirak.

* * * *

Keirak stood under the waterfall in his bathroom and let the warm water wash down his naked body. Even though he had taken a shower earlier, he needed to cool down the desire that consumed him. It had been hours since he saw Kitty, but his body wouldn't listen to reason, and his cock still pulsed hard. He let his hand grip his erection as he started to stroke himself. It had become a nightly ritual, him bringing himself off as he thought of Kitty. He pumped his shaft at a steady pace, taking his time as he pictured what she would look like nude.

He imagined her under the waterfall, her glorious form slick and glistening from the water, the droplets sliding down her body and leaving no part of her untouched. He picked up a faster rhythm and leaned against the rock wall. Her hands ran over her breasts, her nipples hard despite the warm water cascading over her. His orgasm came on quickly, which was not unusual when he thought of her.

He threw his head back and groaned as his seed shot out and landed on the stone wall. He let go of his still hard flesh and hung his head. He breathed deeply, his arousal still raging despite his climax. It was always like this, his body never sated no matter how many times he got off. He wanted one thing—one female, and he wouldn't be sated until he finally claimed her. He quickly rinsed, dried himself off, and sat on the edge of his bed. A knock sounded on his door moments later, and he opened it, bowing his head as Demariak stood on the other side.

"Be at ease."

Keirak stepped aside and let his leader in.

"I just wanted to inform you of the upcoming mission we will be going on. The tribe's supplies are running scarce, and we need to restock."

They spoke for several more minutes, Demariak giving him the journey details as well as how long they would be gone. This journey was good for Kitty as well as himself. Maybe he could get her out of his head while on his journey.

Chapter Three

Kitty helped the other females clear off the tables in the gathering chamber. The warriors went off into the connecting room to speak of the upcoming mission. Normally, the females would pleasure the males after their meals, but tonight, they would be making the journey bags so everything else was put on hold. They cleared everything away, and Kitty watched the older females of the tribe come in with baskets full of supplies. Supper had been uneventful, the normal minus all of the sex and blowjobs. She was used to the orgies, as strange as that was to say, it had become an every day sight.

She had eaten next to Mena, across from Keirak, who tried to not make it obvious that he watched her, but then again, she wouldn't have known that if she hadn't been staring at him. Normally, she would just ignore him, but lately, with her growing feelings, it got harder and harder to ignore his strong presence. She sat on the cool stone floor in a circle with all of the females. She watched in interest as they started to collect pieces of animal hide along with a needle and thick thread. They weaved the needle and thread through the animal hide, the end result being a heavy duty backpack.

"Teetaka vu moohhnie kata?"

Kitty grabbed an animal hide and started to weave the thread through the thick skin. It was harder than it looked, the animal hide so thick you had to practically stab the needle through it.

"She's talking to you Kit."

Kitty looked over at Mena who chuckled to herself as she sewed two pieces of animal hide together. Kitty turned her attention to the olive skinned woman who had spoken. She never really spoke to any of the females of the tribe, little waves and smiles here and there, but mainly she kept to herself. She looked over at Sashaunna, her long black hair and deep amber colored eyes making her beautiful and exotic looking. "Who I'm making it for?" She looked over at Mena and dropped her gaze down at her half made bag.

"Yeah. The women are making a journey bag for one of the males. I'm making Demariak's, and Sashaunna wants to know who you're making yours for."

"Tatttuka vammuna thennala, Icezak."

"She says she's making hers for Icezak."

Kitty looked from Mena to Sashaunna. She envied Mena for how quickly she picked up on the ZorZack language. Kitty seemed to be the only one who was truly an outsider. "Well, I don't know."

"You should make one for Keirak."

She looked over at the fair skinned female called Ashta.

"You can deny it all you want, but everyone can see how the two of you look at each other. I personally think Keirak would be appreciative if you made something for him." Mena spoke without looking up, her full attention on the bag she made.

Kitty ran her hand over the smooth skin of the hide, Keirak's face flashing through her mind. What was the point of hiding her feelings when everyone around her could see them clear as day? She didn't look back up or speak, just finished stitching the hide together. She gazed up when she felt the light touch at her shoulder. Ashta stared at her, her big, pale blue eyes filled with amusement.

"I think he will love it." Ashta dropped her head as she spoke softly, a smile playing on her bow like lips.

* * * *

After an hour of making the bags, Kitty headed to the greenhouse. Over the past year, she routinely went there and tended to the flowers. It really wasn't much work, just taking water from the fountain in the center of the room and watering the plants with it. It was the only room that actually had a view outside, a small opening at the top of the ceiling that let the sun light in. Tucking the journey bag under her arm that she planned to give Keirak, she turned the last corner and made her way through the opening and into the greenhouse.

Tending to the flowers reminded her of when she used to do it back home. At first, it had brought tears to her eyes. After she finished, she made herself comfortable in one of the chairs that had been carved out of a thick tree trunk. She looked at the ceiling, the seven moons shining high above with stars scattered around them. She sat there for a while, just staring at the inky black sky and the blue glow of the moons. She was about to go back to her room when she heard loud and steady footsteps approaching. She looked at the doorway, her heart racing as Keirak walked in.

He was oblivious to her presence as he held a silver glass vase and went toward the flowers. She sat quietly, not moving as he made his way around the flowers, picking the most beautiful and exotic ones. She smiled as he smelled each one before putting them in the vase. It surprised her that he didn't know she was there. She had learned over her time spent with them that the ZorZacks senses were far more advanced than a human. She could tell his concentration was on other things, his mind focused only on the task at hand. After he left, she sat there, her mind churning as to why he would want a vase full of flowers.

She left the garden room and walked through the cold stone hallways and back to her room, her thoughts on Keirak. As she rounded the corner that led to her room, she stopped dead in her tracks at what she saw. On the ground, in front of her door, was a vase filled with flowers. The same vase and the same flowers she had seen Keirak picking just a short time ago. She looked around, hoping to see him, disappointment filling her when she realized she was alone. She walked slowly toward her door and picked up the vase, bringing the flowers to her nose to inhale their sweet scent. She smiled as she turned around again.

Silence and emptiness greeted her. She opened the door and walked inside, setting the flowers on the table by her bed. As she followed her nightly routine, her gaze continually strayed to Keirak's gift. Who was she kidding? Everyone could clearly see the feelings she tried to deny. She climbed onto her bed, lying on her side so that she could see the flowers. Tomorrow, she decided. Tomorrow she would tell Keirak exactly how she felt. She just hoped she didn't live to regret it.

* * * *

When she woke the following morning, the flowers were the first thing that caught her eyes. She performed her morning ritual and had one plan in mind—find Keirak and tell him her feelings before he left for his journey. She slipped on a light blue dress that held a silvery iridescent glow. She left her hair down, the blond waves long enough that they touched her hips. She looked at herself one last time in the polished metal before heading toward the door, gripping the handle, and taking a deep breath. She opened it, her eyes growing big at who stood on the other side. Keirak stared at her, his huge, leather clad legs braced apart, his chest bare and stunning. She swallowed at the sight of him, determined not to lose her nerve.

"Hi. What are you doing here?" He watched her with half-lidded eyes, his muscles bulging and flexing beneath his golden skin. His platinum blond hair was disheveled—a really good look on him. The sharp edges of a tattoo peeked through the top of his leather pants, and she idly wondered where the rest went...wondered what the rest looked like. She cleared her throat, realizing he hadn't answered her question. "I'm sorry, I'm being rude. Do you want to come in?" She had never invited him into her room, but things were different now.

"I must leave for a journey with the other warriors."

"I know, Mena told me. When will you have to leave?"

"At sunset."

"So soon?" Even though she knew he had to leave, actually hearing it out loud seemed to make it that much harder. "I have something for you." She turned to grab the journey bag she made and went back to the door. His brows bunched together in confusion as she presented him with the cloth-enclosed journey bag. He stared at it for several seconds, his eyes going from the bag to her. She lifted it up, his big hands encasing hers before sliding it out. Her heart started to race where their skin touched, an electrical charge that shot straight between her legs and had her clenching her thighs together. She stepped back and watched him, hoping he would like what she made for him, but bracing herself if he didn't.

Confusion still covered his features when he pulled the cloth back and stared at the bag. He didn't say anything for a long time, and she grew uncomfortable at the silence. "I'm not very good at putting things together, so if you don't like it, that's okay." She was embarrassed that he didn't like it—at least that's what she took his silence as. She glanced up at him and gasped as his body came forward and crowded hers. He was so close she could smell the purely male scent that enveloped him…it intoxicated her. She craned her head back, his smooth, tawny chest in her view, the need to run her hands over the firm skin almost overpowering her. "What are you doing?" She stuttered the words as she took an involuntary step back and looked into his neon green stare.

"You made me a journey bag?"

"Yes. The women were sitting around, and they said I should make one for someone, so I made one for you. If you don't like it I understand." Excitement and a touch of anxiety coursed through her as she stared at him. Her eyes went wide as his big hand gently caressed her face and his lips slanted over hers.

His tongue ran along the seam of her lips, teasing and tantalizing her. She opened her mouth more in shock than anything else, but as soon as his tongue moved along hers, she was lost in pleasure. He kept one hand on her cheek as the other one slid down to her hip. He gripped her side, bringing her body flush with his, the hard bulge of his erection pressing erotically against her belly.

Their tongues moved together in an intimate caress, the sensual glide making her wet and needy. She moved her hands tentatively to his chest, his growl of approval fueling her arousal and giving her the courage she needed. She ran her hands over the smooth skin, the muscles tight and hard and filled with so much power.

She slid her hands up to his shoulders and wrapped them around his neck, pulling his mouth closer. He walked her backward until the back of her legs hit the edge of the bed. She sat down, their mouths never breaking as he moved with her. She spread her legs to accommodate his large frame and groaned when he pushed his erection against her pussy.

Her heart rate picked up as he started a slow grind against her vagina, his cock moving against her clit and sending electrical currents all the way through her. His shaft was big and thick as it pressed against her slit. He broke their kiss and moved down to her neck, biting gently and then licking the pleasure-pain away.

"I have wanted you from the moment I saw you."

His whispered words sent shock waves through her vagina, and it clenched as if trying to grip what it really wanted. She was surprised by his admission. "You have?" He pulled his head back and framed her face with his hands, his green stare intense, yet caring. A slow, sensual smile played across his lips, and he brought his mouth down to hers for a slow kiss.

"I have, so very, very much."

She smiled against his lips and closed her eyes. "I want you, too. I didn't want to, I fought it, but in the end, I can't deny my feelings for you any longer. I wanted to find you before you left to tell you."

He pulled back and sat on his haunches and stared at her. "You did?"

She nodded and gasped as he pushed her back on the bed, his body covering her as his mouth took possession of her lips. He stroked her hair, his mouth trailing kissing down the side of her neck and over her collar bone. He moved his mouth over the top of her breast, his hot air caressing her skin even through the fabric of her gown. She wanted his mouth there so badly it hurt.

His lips hovered precariously close to her stiff nipple, and she knew she should be embarrassed by the way it stabbed through the material. All she would have to do was arch her spine, just a little bit, and her nipple would rub against his lips. A warm gush of wetness slid out of her body at the illicit thought. He growled deeply, the sound vibrating straight through her and tingling all of her erogenous zones.

"I can smell the sweet nectar that spills from you. I want to lap it up before I stab my cock deep inside of you."

She breathed heavily, every word he spoke bringing her desire so high she didn't know if it would ever come down. He gripped the hem of her dress and slid it up and over her head. He tossed it on the ground, staring down at her and causing her to shiver in delight. He moved down her body, his hands rubbing over every inch of her exposed skin in the process. He gripped her calves, staring up at her as he gently pulled them open.

He settled between her thighs, his body so big it dwarfed hers and made her feel petite and feminine. Her clit tingled with every breath he took, the current of air gently wafting over the engorged bead. His hands smoothed over her thighs, getting closer and closer to what really ached. His big hands framed her pussy, his thumbs gently pulling her labia's apart and blowing hot air over her saturated folds.

"You are so beautiful."

She dropped her head on the bed and closed her eyes as his tongue swirled around her opening. She felt his tongue flatten out as he dragged it up to her clit, sucking the pulsating bead into his mouth as he moaned. The vibrations had her arching her back in pleasure. She opened her eyes and looked down at him, the very sight of what he was doing an aphrodisiac.

He took his thumb and forefinger and framed her clit, pulling her lips apart so that the nub stood out alone. He stopped sucking and looked into her eyes, never breaking contact as he dipped his head back down and twirled his tongue around it. Her mouth fell open as intense pleasure pulsated through her, bringing her climax to the brink of explosion.

She felt his finger probe at her pussy hole, and she lifted her hips up in hopes of it sliding inside of her. In the next instant, he covered her clit with his hot mouth, his tongue swirling and lapping at it as his finger slid into her gently. Her orgasm slammed through her so forcefully she couldn't catch her breath. He didn't let up his ministrations as he teased her now clenching pussy and sucked harder. She screamed out her release, spearing her hands through her hair and trying desperately to suck in air.

She squeezed her eyes shut tightly, letting the after pleasure burn of her climax wash through her as her gave her clit one last lick before pulling away. She opened her eyes, feeling sleepy and sated. Her orgasm only seemed to intensify her arousal, and she spread her legs wider, hoping he'd take the hint. She could see how hard he was, could see how much he wanted her, but he didn't move.

After a minute of silence, she pulled herself up, suddenly feeling very shy. His eyes were downcast, his fists clenching and unclenching at his sides as he ground his teeth. "Keirak? Is everything okay?" She reached her hand out and tentatively touched his arm. He flinched in response and she immediately withdrew it, confusion and hurt resonating within her. "What's wrong? Don't you want this? I know I do."

"We need to stop."

What? Could she have heard him right? He actually wanted to stop? He actually *could* stop? He moved and sat on the edge of the bed, resting his massive forearms on his thighs and breathing out deeply. "We don't have to. I want this, I want you, Keirak." She didn't move any closer as she rested her back against the wall. He was strong and muscular everywhere, the tendons and sinew evident even in his back. She dropped her eyes and stared at the dark ink of his tattoo that snaked from beneath his pants.

She absently lifted her arm and ran her fingers over the dark lines. He stiffened again beneath her touch, and she dropped her hand. Could she have been so wrong about how he felt? Did he not feel the same for her? Was she not experienced enough? Too human? The questions bouncing in her mind brought her down, but she didn't let it show. "I'm sorry, I didn't mean to."

"Don't ever apologize to me, *fallina*. It's not you, it's me."

She snorted, actually snorted at his *cliché* comment. She leaned back and stared at the ceiling. He looked over his shoulder at her, his brows knitted in clear confusion. "Sorry, it's just that guys say that exact statement where I'm from when they are trying to let a girl down easy." He turned his big body all the way around, his expression almost sad as he stared at her.

"You don't truly believe that do you?"

"I don't know what to believe anymore. Listen, just forget I said anything." She felt like an ass, a complete and total ass. She dropped her head, "Maybe you should g…" The last word left on a gasp as he pulled her down the bed and covered her body with his once again in a matter of seconds. He stared down at her, his eyes roaming over her face as his hand played with a strand of her hair.

"I love you so much my heart aches. I tried to keep my distance—thought it would be best, but I can't deny my feelings. I am rough and scarred, Kitty, a hardened warrior that doesn't deserve you. I want to be soft and gentle with you, the kind of male you deserve, but I fear I won't be able to accomplish that. Look at how I just acted with you, ravished your body so selfishly."

She stared at him with an open mouth, not even knowing how to go explain that he certainly *did* ravish her body, but she liked it—a lot. He had spoken softly, so gentle and caring, the complete opposite of the persona he displayed—or tried to display. His eyes continued to move over her face, as if imprinting every dip and hollow. She certainly hadn't expected that from him, but as his words played over and over in her mind, she had the strong need to say it back. "I love you, too."

A look of relief crossed his features and she leaned up and pressed her lips to his. The kiss was soft, almost tentative in its nature. "I want you as you are. I want the strong, hard warrior that I see now. What I want, what I need is *you*, Keirak, just as you are." He rolled onto his back and brought her across his chest. She rested her head over his heart, the strong and steady beat sending soothing waves through her. "I wanted to keep my distance, too, thought it would be better in the end if I did, but the heart knows what it truly needs, and what I truly need is you."

* * * *

They stayed like that, in a comfortable silence, her atop his chest as he ran his hands over her back. Her eyes started to grow heavy, the rhythmic beat of his heart a steady lullaby.

"I must leave, *fallina*. I have to prepare for the journey, but will you meet me before I go?"

"Of course. Where, when?" Her words were soft and sleepy, her eyes half-lidded as she dragged her fingers lightly over his chest.

"We will meet at the main tunnel, just before sunset tonight."

She sat up, her legs spreading as she straddled his hips and looked down at him. His hands gripped her waist as he thrusted his hips up. His cock pressed along her slit, and she swallowed at his length and girth. "How long will you be gone?" She inhaled as he pushed up again, his hardness hitting her clit and making her wet in a matter of seconds.

"I have wanted to do that for the past year."

His voice was deep and filled with arousal, his hands gripping and releasing her hips in rhythm to his thrusting. "Don't distract me." She moaned as he set a steady rhythm. His cock pushed against her labia and caused a delicious sensation to bloom within her.

"You feel so good on top of me."

She closed her eyes when his hands skated across her breasts, his palms rasping over her nipples and making them bead in wanton pleasure. "That makes me…" She didn't finish her words, couldn't finish them as his hands continued to move across her nipple.

"That makes you feel what?" He growled deeply, the sound filled with arousal that matched hers.

"It makes me wet." She opened her eyes, her face heating at what she'd just said. She never spoke this way and it was embarrassing. "It feels so good."

"Not nearly as good as it feels for me, my love."

His hands moved up to the sides of her neck and brought her down for another intimate kiss. He broke the kiss, their heavy breathing mingling as they caught their breath. "Your nectar smells like the blooming after a rainfall, it's intoxicating."

He kissed her on the lips, nothing deep or penetrating, just a sweet kiss that left her frustrated. "You have to go, don't you?"

"I do. I shall only be gone for a few weeks, although it will feel like eternity."

"Where will you guys go?" She pulled back and rolled off of him, knowing that if she didn't they would never leave the room.

"Our supplies are running low. We must also go to several other tribes and trade goods with them."

"I wish you didn't have to go." She sat on the edge of the bed and felt his hand run down her back.

"I wish I didn't have to either, but I am second in command and must."

They said their goodbyes, Keirak holding the journey bag as they kissed one last time. He started to leave but stopped and turned around. "Thank you for this." He gestured to the journey bag and smiled. He took her hand and kissed it, bringing it to rest over his heart as he stared at her for a suspended second before he let it go.

She shut the door and leaned back against it, her emotions swirling wildly inside of her.

Chapter Four

Kitty stood in a straight line with the other females as she looked at the warriors across from them. Each one looked as if they were ready to do battle, weapons hanging off of their leathers and fierce expressions covering their faces. She stood directly across from Keirak, his eyes never leaving her face as Demariak spoke about the plans for the mission.

Right before everyone had lined up, Keirak had given her back the journey bag. She was confused to the why of it but didn't question him as everyone took their place. The room grew silent as Sashaunna walked up to Icezak, dropped her head, and held the journey bag out to him. She spoke in the ZorZack language and stepped back in line after he took the bag.

Each woman did this to a warrior until the only couple left was Kitty and Keirak. She knew everyone watched intently, which amplified the awkwardness of the whole situation. She may have been living here for a year, but for a good portion of that time she had done everything in her power to avoid anything that related to this world. Now, she wished she had taken a stronger interest in their culture so she didn't look like such a fool.

Her heart beat rapidly as she stared at Keirak. His green stare was intense and knowing, as if he understood exactly how uncomfortable this was for her. She stepped forward until they stood only a foot apart. Electricity and desire sparked between them, a connection that they both shared and she couldn't even begin to explain. She tore her eyes away from him and looked at the ground. She heard him swallow and offered the bag to him. One of his hands landed on top of hers, the other below it so that the warmth from his touch covered her completely.

"Thank you, *fallina*."

None of the other warriors had spoken when they received their bags, and she looked up to stare at him. His head was downcast slightly, his eyes half-lidded so that all she could see were two neon green slits. It was like they were the only two people in the whole room.

"What does that mean?"

He stared at her, a small smile covering his full lips. "I will tell you once I have returned." He leaned in close to her ear and whispered, "I will tell you when I am buried so deep inside of you we are one."

Her eyes grew wide at his illicit words, and she quickly looked around. The females and warriors were in intimate embraces, some of them moving toward the shadowed crevasses. Their hands moved over each other's body, telling of exactly what they would be doing in those corners.

She looked back into his face, her pussy going instantly wet and her nipples stabbing through her dress. He growled low in his throat and gripped her arm, all but dragging her toward one of those darkened, secluded areas. As they made their way toward the shadows, she could hear panting and moaning as the warriors and their partners "relieved" their tension before the mission.

"What are you doing?"

He didn't say anything as he walked behind a large rock that was cloaked in shadows and pressed her against the wall. He brought his body flush against hers, and she gasped in delight. He placed his large hand behind her head and brought his mouth down to hers. He kissed her with such a fierce passion that it left her breathless. She stood there, body tense, as he ran his tongue over her lips, tempting her to open them. She closed her eyes and opened her mouth as she moaned.

His tongue speared in and stroked over hers, his hands smoothing behind her and pressing against her lower back. He slowly moved toward her ass, cupping each cheek and bringing her groin flush against his erection. Moisture slipped out of her vagina as the hard length of him pressed against her belly. Her nipples rubbed against his hard, smooth chest, the feeling causing goose bumps to form over her flesh. She broke the kiss and breathed out, their mouths mere inches apart.

"What are you doing?" He buried his face in her neck and she felt his tongue lick up the side. She shivered and gripped his shoulders, her nails pressing into his flesh as a growl erupted from his throat. He brought his hands up to cup her breasts, his thumbs rasping over her engorged nipples until they were rock hard.

"What I've been craving all day."

His touch started off soft and gentle, but soon became frantic and passion filled. His lips slanted over hers again, his hand running over every inch of her body, leaving nothing untouched. She opened her legs wider, his large body moving in closer, his cock pressing more firmly into her. His hand moved between their bodies—the warmth of his skin already seeping into her. He moved it lower to the spot where she wanted him most. He cupped her vagina and pressed his thumb against her clit, the slight pressure edging her closer to climax.

She didn't want him to stop, actually wanted to see how much more he could give. She gasped when his fingers ran up and down her slit, the material of the dress pressing into her and causing an incredible friction against her sensitive lips. Her gown was saturated from her juices, his fingers still moving ruthlessly against her flesh and bringing her closer to the brink of climax.

He dropped to his knees, hiking her dress up and lifting one of her legs over his shoulder. He stared up at her, not moving, not breathing, as if he was waiting for her to give permission. At her nod, he licked and sucked at her folds, his finger moving to strum her clit and bringing her closer and closer to what she wanted…needed.

She gripped the rock behind her, leaning her head back and closing her eyes as she breathed in deeply. She looked down again, Keirak's head hidden under her dress, the sounds of wet sucking filling her ears. She opened her mouth on a silent scream as his fingers slid into her vagina. She was so close, so…close.

She moaned loudly, her climax starting at her toes and traveling through her body so quickly she didn't have the strength to stay upright. Before her rubbery legs gave out, Keirak was in front of her, his body pressed against hers as his mouth covered her lips. She tasted herself on his tongue, a flavor that lit up her senses and had them both groaning. She wanted to give him the kind of pleasure he gave her, wanted him to know how good he made her feel.

She dropped to her knees, looking up at the startled expression that crossed his face. She didn't speak or wait for his permission, just started to unlace his leathers and pull them apart. She reached in, pulling out his huge cock, his flesh so hot and hard it had her swallowing in appreciation. She held his erection in her hand, her eyes widening at how truly big he was. His shaft was smooth and flawless, the head swollen and red, the slit already seeping pre-cum and making her mouth water.

"Kitty?"

He spoke her name on a groan, and it gave her the courage she needed. She ran her tongue over the slit, moaning at the salty, male taste he provided. She wrapped her tongue around the engorged head, running her tongue over the crown and back to the slit where she gently pushed against it. She slid her mouth down on him, opening her throat and taking a little bit more of him inside her mouth. Her hand gripped the middle of his erection and gently stroked it. He was so thick she couldn't touch her fingers as she gripped his cock tighter and picked up a faster motion. Soon, she was moving her head up and down, her saliva giving her the needed lubrication to make the ride smooth.

His hands framed her head, his hips slightly thrusting in and out of her mouth as he groaned and moaned above her. She couldn't get very much of his cock into her mouth, but the erotic noises he was making gave her the encouragement she needed to keep going. Salty male essence seeped continuously out of his slit, and she knew he was close. In the next instant, he tried to pull away but she held onto him tight. She bobbed her head faster on his cock, knowing he was about to go off.

He groaned loudly, and she moaned against his shaft, finally tasting his thick cum slide down her throat. It continued to pulse out of him, filling her mouth, filling her senses. He gripped her hair, the slight sting the action caused giving her pleasure and making her pussy seep. When his orgasm finally let up, he pulled away and helped her off the ground. He cradled her body close to his and whispering words in his language to her.

"I love you, *fallina*. I'm going to miss you."

She smiled against his chest, knowing that she was already too deep into this to turn away unscathed. "I love you, too. I wish you didn't have to go."

"Me too."

Chapter Five

Keirak and the other warriors marched through the heavy foliage of the jungle, the branches and leaves slapping against their leather clad bodies as the noise bounced off the trees. The closest village was a day's hike away—a small tribe known as the *Monna He*. They visited this particular tribe countless times throughout the years, exchanging goods and weapons and resting their weary bodies. The *Monna Hes* were a gentle and peaceful tribe but strong allies nonetheless.

Keirak and the other warriors had been walking for hours, many of the males telling stories of their latest female conquests. The stories were ritual during these trips, many of his brethren sharing the same female, many picking up pointers for when they returned and needed to be sated. They were excited to visit the *Monna He*—their females slender with fire red hair and ample breasts. The men were built the same way, more toned, but slender nonetheless. They also carried the distinctive fire colored hair, and so that is how their tribe's name, *Monna He*—fire people—came to be.

They were about five hours from the small tribe, the atmosphere and the creatures of the jungle silent as they trekked forward. He wished the beasts of the jungle would come out. He wanted a fight, a good brawl that would work off some of the testosterone that fueled his arousal. His dick was still pressed tightly against his leathers, an uncomfortable feeling when trying to walk through the thick foliage.

"I can't wait to bury my cock deep inside of Eyessa." Icezak slapped Keirak on the back, a wide smile covering his face as he walked toward the front of the group.

"I thought you and Sashaunna had a thing going on?" Drayden's voice boomed through the night.

Icezak shrugged his broad shoulders as he slashed his *Fidorina* blade though the branches. The blade was three feet long and sharpened to a deadly point, perfect for the thick leaves and branches the forest produced. The moon shone off the metal as it peeked from the thick covering of trees above them. Keirak looked back at Drayden who wore that ever present hard set. There was something under his persona though, something that hinted to why he cared about Icezak and Sashaunna.

"We are not mated so I am free to do as I wish. She's a good fuck though."

"So you use her for your amusement only?"

Icezak stopped and turned around, anger sparking in his blue eyes. "You know better than that. If anyone would be using a female for their amusement it would be you."

A fight was brewing, but just as the two stepped close to each other, Demariak stepped in between them, not saying a word, a fierce look on his face. They knew better than to go against their leader, and so the fight ceased. Keirak looked at Drayden, confused as to why he would care.

Drayden was a fine warrior, their most ruthless when it came to the hunt, but he always kept his distance. Of course, he took females to bed, but Keirak heard the females speak of how unemotional he was. He finished with them almost as soon as he started. Even after the females knew this, they still flocked toward him, the power he emitted like a drug they needed. They started walking again, their pace picking up as tension coated the air.

"Who have you left in charge of the tribe, my lord?" Demariak didn't turn around as he too sliced through branches, grunting with the effort.

"Rhyson. It will give him a chance to prove himself, although I have left Adriak and Merak to watch over him."

Surprise filtered through Keirak as he wondered why Demariak had chosen him to look after the tribe given. Rhyson thought more with his dick than his brain. Whenever anyone wondered about Rhyson's whereabouts, all they needed to do was see which female was missing, or *females* in most cases. All the warriors had "healthy" appetites when it came to bedding females, but Rhyson far surpassed all of them.

"Maybe a little bit of power will make him somewhat responsible."

Keirak highly doubted it.

* * * *

It had been two days and, already, Kitty was miserable. She hadn't realized how much she would miss Keirak. She walked to the hot springs, a cave with several heated, natural pools and a waterfall. It was nice and relaxing, and she hoped the warm water might control some of the lust that brewed inside her. Before she even rounded the corner to enter the cave, she heard low male and female groans. She stopped and turned around, not even about to go in there when it was obvious what was going on. She ran right into a thick chest, gasping as she stumbled back. "I'm sorry." She looked into a face that held nothing but amusement.

"I'm not."

She gripped her towel—really just a strip of cloth—in her hands tightly and looked around. She knew this man, not very well, but his reputation was notorious in the tribe.

"I don't think we've properly met." He took hold of her hand and brought it to his lips, laying a gentle kiss on her skin. "I'm Rhyson."

"I know." She swallowed again, trying to look around his massive body and thinking of how to leave without seeming rude. He was a huge man, not as tall as Keirak, but definitely packing a lot of muscle. It also didn't help that he had a giant serpent tattooed on his body.

The monster wrapped its fearsome body around the entire length of one of his arms, the head and dagger like teeth ending on the opposite shoulder. The beast's eyes were silver and stared right at her, the mercury colored orbs almost glowing in their intensity.

"Really? Tell me, are they all good?"

Many of the men and women in the tribe spoke English, not the best, but enough that they could communicate. Rhyson spoke it fluently, with only the slightest accent laced in his deep voice.

"Was what all good?" She took her hand from his grasp and took a step back. He smiled slowly.

"What you have heard about me."

"I don't think you want to know."

His laugh was low and deep, his eyes never leaving her face. "I can't believe I haven't seen more of you around. A shame really."

His eyes roamed over her body and that was when she remembered the leather bathing suit she had on. The women of the tribe swam nude, no surprise there, but she didn't follow in their footsteps. So, with Mena's help, she had crafted what resembled a bathing suit out of animal hide. It wasn't anything fancy, but covered her parts so she didn't feel like an exhibitionist. She tightened her 'towel' around her body and glared at him. "Is there anything in particular I can help you with?"

"Hmmm…I can think of many things I need your *help* with."

She laughed at how ridiculous he sounded. He truly was trying to seduce her. "I'm sorry, but I'm taken."

"Are you?" He did another slow sweep of her body with his eyes.

"Yes, I am. I'm also rude, a recluse, and very unattainable. You picked the wrong woman to charm."

"Ah, so you admit I'm charming?"

A wide smile covered his face, and she couldn't help but smile. "Absolutely not, but don't you have a young girl to corrupt or something?"

"I only go after the fine aged females. The younger ones are much to wild for my taste."

She found that very hard to believe but didn't bother saying anything more. Female giggles and deep male laughs sounded behind her, and she looked over her shoulder. She recognized the men, Merak and Adriak, and the lone woman sandwiched between them, Talliya. The woman looked worn out, her long blond hair soaked and pasted to her curvy nude body. The twins held her up, their hands running over every part of her flesh that they could reach.

Even though Kitty was used to this kind of behavior from the ZorZacks, it didn't mean she enjoyed watching it. Everywhere she looked, every corner she turned, seemed to have grinding bodies doing some kind of sexual act. She wasn't a prude by any means, but she wasn't into watching porno all the time. She didn't miss how Rhyson eyed Talliya, and she was thankful for small favors that he became distracted. She took the opportunity to slip by him, but not before he grabbed her hand, stopping her dead in her tracks.

"Leaving so soon? I thought we could take a dip together."

"No, thank you."

"Are you sure? We can get to know each other better?"

She shook her head and pulled her arm away.

"If you knew what was good for you, you'd leave her be." Merak walked up to Rhyson, their feet inches apart as they stared at each other. The room suddenly filled with tension, and Kitty looked between the two of them.

"Maybe you should worry about your own female."

"She isn't your female, Rhyson."

"And she's yours?"

Merak turned her way and stared at her, his burnt amber eyes holding her gaze intently. "She's neither one of ours. She's claimed by Keirak. If you paid more attention, instead of burying your cock in any available female, you would have known that."

She took a step back as she noticed Rhyson's fist clenching and his jaw tensing. Merak had a smirk on his face, but his body was coiled tight, ready for whatever happened.

"I see no mark, no metal adorning her. When I see some kind of proof, then I will keep my distance. Until then, all is fair." He turned and looked at Kitty, a slow smile spreading across his face before he stormed past Merak, shoulder slamming into his as he made his way to the hot springs.

The silence was deafening, just a lot of breathing and testosterone that filled the small tunnel. "Well." She cleared her throat but didn't know what else to say.

"If he bothers you again, tell me." Merak turned and looked down at her, his face a mask of fury that she knew wasn't directed toward her. "It is better if I diffuse this right away. If Keirak finds out about this, Rhyson will regret it. I have my honor to uphold and promised Demariak I would look after things. Rhyson is a strong warrior but wild."

He turned and walked away with his brother and Talliya, leaving Kitty standing there alone, not knowing what had just happened.

Chapter Six

Keirak sat around a large fire getting drunk off the juice of a *Koolna* plant. He took another swig from the blown glass jar, the potent liquid hot like the flames that burned in front of him. Icezak sat next to him, Eyessa in his lap, her red hair the same color as the fire. She sat there, completely nude, but so did every female that was around. He watched Icezak suck her deep red nipples into his mouth, her moans loud and ringing through the air. Keirak was horny. Not because he watched Icezak tease and fondle the female, but because he constantly thought of Kitty.

He closed his eyes as he drank deeply from the jar—the liquid making him feel intoxicated. He pictured Kitty in his mind, her soft and supple body beneath his, her perfectly rounded breasts in his mouth. His cock strained against his leathers, and he shifted uncomfortably. *This is hell.* He opened his eyes and looked over at Drayden who also had a female straddled across his lap. Her back was toward Keirak and her ass was spread wide. Her pussy was soaking wet and glistened off the fire light. Drayden's hands moved to grip both globes of her ass, moving in and sliding two fingers inside of her.

Keirak looked away, disgusted with himself for even looking. Before Kitty had come into his life, he fucked two, sometimes three women a day, but now, he couldn't even stomach the idea of another woman. His already hard cock grew stiffer as he watched his fellow warriors tease the women, and he felt disgusted by his body's reaction. He threw his head back and downed the last of the liquid, the *Koolna* juice settling in his belly and starting a slow burn. He was about to get up and grab another bottle when a hand ran across his shoulder and stopped him.

"It has been too long."

He didn't need to look behind him to know who spoke. Iteena sat beside him, a full bottle of *Koolna* juice in her hand and a smile on her face. He knew her well, fucked her every time he had visited her village, but even thinking about that now had him feeling ashamed.

She was attractive, her breasts huge mounds that swayed and bounced with every step and her pussy shaved bare for all to see. As he looked at her, she didn't spark any kind of lust inside of him. She handed him the bottle and sat next to him, leaning back on her hands so that her breasts were displayed.

"I've missed you, *leano*."

He hated it when she called him that, a stupid endearment that made his teeth gnash together. "Have you?" He took another sip, his attention of the dancing flames in front of him.

"I have."

Her whispered words were right next to his ear, and he pulled away, shaking his head. "Not this time. Iteena I have a female."

"Did she travel with you? I do not see any females of your tribe. I won't tell if you won't."

She was trying to seduce him, but Kitty filled his every thought, made every emotion he had so much more powerful. Iteena seemed insubstantial compared to her. "I am sure Icezak or Draydon—or both—will be happy to fuck you."

"I have no doubts about that. I actually plan on that later, but I haven't been able to get you out of my mind since the last time you visited."

He didn't bother responding, just watched the fire. He heard her sigh before she ran her hand across his back and walked away. She gave up much easier than he expected, and he was thankful.

He finished off the second bottle just as more and more female moans sounded all around him. He scrubbed a hand across his face and made his way toward his sleeping chamber. He passed Demariak's hut, his leader's deep, even breathing letting him know his king already slept. His hut was on the other side of the camp, away from everyone else which is why he requested it. He didn't want to hear the heavy panting, the moaning, or the screams that would last all night.

He was drunk, completely and utterly drunk, and he didn't care. His senses were dulled and fatigue weighed heavily on him. He hoped his cock would give up on tormenting him for the night. He stumbled into his hut and made his way over to the pallet in the corner. He let himself fall onto it, the plush stuffing under the animal hide breaking his fall. He lay on his back, staring at the straw and hardened clay ceiling, his beauty's face flashing through his mind. He closed his eyes, welcoming the alcohol-induced sleep that swept through him.

* * * *

Keirak opened his eyes, the edges of his chamber hazy, as if a veil were all around him. He stared into Kitty's ecstasy filled face as she stared down at him, her wet pussy sliding over his leg as she straddled him. He knew it was a dream, but he had no plans on waking anytime soon. She ran her hands over him and murmured her encouragements. Even though he knew this was a dream, it felt weird, *she* felt weird.

He rubbed his eyes, gently pushing her away and sitting up. He felt so dizzy and discombobulated. Her hands smoothed over his back, her lips pressing against his shoulder, her tongue sliding along his jaw. He turned his head and stared at Kitty, her hair flashing from blond to red and back to blond again. He squeezed his eyes shut. He felt her move onto his lap, the smell of her wet sex filling his senses.

Her mouth slanted over his, her tongue sliding along the seam of his lips and causing him to snap his eyes open. She didn't taste or smell like Kitty. He moved her off of him and shook his head. He closed his eyes again, his head pounding fiercely as he ran a hand across his face.

"What's wrong, *leano*?"

He snapped his eyes open and looked to the side, Iteena's naked body and red hair filling all of his senses. She smiled and lifted her hand to touch him but he quickly moved away, shaking his head. "What are you doing in my hut?"

"You are being very rude, *leano*. I know you want me. I can see the evidence through your leathers." She ran her hands across her breasts, pulling one to her mouth and wrapping her tongue around the nipple. "I can finish you off if you like. Maybe wrap my mouth around that huge cock of yours."

He shook his head, pushing her hands away when she tried to fondle him.

"Just leave."

"Why are you so cold all of the sudden?"

Rage swirled and churned inside of him, but he knew he was to blame. True, he had been drunk and thought it a dream, but he should have known better, should have been able to tell it wasn't Kitty. He turned his head, not caring that she gasped at his cold expression. "Even after I told you I didn't want you, you had to be persistent."

"I came in to see if you changed your mind. You were mumbling, and I noticed how engorged you cock was. I took it that you wanted me." He would have felt bad for the anger he directed toward her, but he knew she could be cold and calculating, and he had no doubts she knew exactly what she had done.

"I thought you were another. I pictured another. Please, just leave."

She huffed and stood, glaring down at him with her hands on her hips before turning and storming out of the hut. He fell back on his pallet, throwing an arm over his eyes and wishing he could just see Kitty, his sweet, sweet, *fallina*.

Chapter Seven

Kitty walked to Mena's room with a bouquet of freshly picked flowers in hand. A week already passed, and she was getting more and more anxious to see Keirak. She stopped in front of the huge door, the ZorZacks history carved into the wood. She knocked, hearing Mena's soft voice call her in a moment later. She opened the door, the lighting low and the smell of something exotic in the air. "Where are you? I can barely see anything."

"Shhh, Nea finally went to sleep."

"Sorry," Kitty whispered as she gently closed the door and walked to where Mena lay in bed. "Is everything okay? You don't look very well."

"I don't feel very well. I think I ate something that didn't agree with me. It might have been those little, green colored beans I ate for lunch, they packed quite a kick."

"Here, I thought you might like these."

"Thank you, you're so sweet. Can you put them on the table over there? I'd do it myself, but every time I get up I feel nauseous."

Mena looked pretty pale, and that worried Kitty. "Do you want me to take Nea for a while so you can get some rest?"

"Nah, it's okay. I actually feel a lot better than I did." She rubbed her belly, wincing slightly in the process.

"Is everything okay with the baby?"

"Yeah, the baby is just acting wild today. I don't think the beans agreed with him either."

"Him?" They didn't have the kind of technology that allowed them to see the baby's sex on this world, but it was cute how Mena called the baby "him."

"I'm pretty sure it's a boy. I mean, I have been having these crazy dreams lately about the baby, and it's always a boy." She smiled and started to sit up.

"No, don't move. I'll let you rest, but if you want me to watch Nea just let me know. You look worn out."

"Geez, thanks." Mena laughed quietly but the humor didn't quite reach her eyes. "It's not just me not feeling well. I kind of miss Demariak, too. We have never been away from each other this long."

"Don't worry yourself. He'll be back in no time at all." She still hadn't told Mena about her feelings toward Keirak, but she wasn't going to spill them now, not when Mena looked so tired. "I'll come by tomorrow and see how you're doing, okay?" Mena nodded, sliding down the bed again and letting out a deep breath in the process. "Feel better, okay?" Kitty let herself out, making sure to shut the door as quietly as possible. She was worried about Mena, she had never seen her look so tired and pale before.

The caves were pretty quiet, so she took the opportunity to change into her bathing suit in her room and head to the hot springs. Her steps were light and quiet as she entered the steamy, humid cave that held four bubbling hot springs. One of them was as big as a residential swimming pool, the other three the size of hot tubs. She set her towel on the ledge and tested the water with her toe. The water felt warm and bubbly, and she stepped in and sat down, leaning her head against the smooth rock and closing her eyes. She breathed in as the water lapped at her neck, the warmth doing nothing to help the arousal that still plagued her.

She slowly came awake, her body so relaxed that her mind was a little hazy. She rubbed her eyes and gasped when it brushed against a foot. She snapped her eyes open, her heart in her throat as she looked at Rhyson. He wore an amused smile on his face. She gaped at him and moved to the far corner of the hot spring. "You scared the crap out of me."

"I apologize." He said the words clearly, but the expression on his face showed how little he meant them.

She looked around, not wanting to seem rude but very uncomfortable that a naked warrior sat in the same hot springs as her. "You're naked." It was an obvious and stupid statement, but it just rolled off her tongue, and her face immediately reddened.

"I know." He braced his arms on the ledge behind him, his muscles bulging out as he stared at her with a look that could only be described as hungry.

"I was just about to get out."

"So soon?"

She took note of his serpent tattoo again, the creature looking at her as if it were actually alive. She squinted at it, not knowing if the heat made her see things or if his tattoo had moved positions. She remembered just last week the head was wrapped around his neck, its body curling around one of his arms. Today though, the head and upper body seemed lower on his chest, as if the thing had crawled over his skin. She quickly looked back at his face.

"So, how was your day?"

"Fine." She felt uncomfortable and embarrassed.

"Good, that's very good. Do you have plans for tonight?"

"Yes." She spat the word out, knowing she didn't have a damn thing to do tonight.

"Really? You have to eat though, right? Maybe you would like to accompany me in a private meal? "

"Thanks, but no thank you."

"Why is it you dislike me so much when you hardly know me?"

A sad look crossed his features, but she didn't fall into his trap. "It isn't that I dislike you, it's just that, well, I have heard the stories about you, and I'm also taken."

"Ah, by the great Keirak? Then again, you don't know that much about him now, do you?"

"What are you talking about?" She glared at him, about to defend the man she loved if Rhyson so much as said one negative thing.

"What? He has never spoken of his past? He has never told you about *his* reputation amongst the tribe?" Rhyson ran a tanned hand across his jaw before he leaned his head back and closed his eyes, clicking his tongue in the process.

Keirak had never told her about himself, but it wasn't like either of them had been very open about their lives. "If he chooses to tell me about his past then he will."

"Well, it isn't my story to tell, but before you judge me on what you have *heard*, ask your mate about his past indiscretions, you might be surprised." He still had his head back and his eyes closed, but he chuckled deeply. "Have a wonderful night, sweet Kitty."

She slipped out of the water and wrapped the towel around her dripping body. She didn't even want to think about Keirak doing the kinds of things she heard Rhyson did. She didn't want to picture Keirak with another woman, let alone a harem. The very idea of him wrapped around a woman, bringing her the kind of pleasure he gave her had her heart clenching.

Rhyson looked at her, his expression stoic as he spoke softly. "I'm not so bad, Kitty. I hope you can see that soon."

* * * *

Keirak stood at the front of his group, slashing through the thick leaves that helped to obscure the blazing sun. Guilt and disgust still overwhelmed him, as well as a big dose of rage. His brethren were smart enough to stay far back from him as he tore through the branches. They had been on their trek for days now, not even the sound of nearby creatures breaking up the monotony of their journey. The jungle seemed void of life, not even wind moved against his face.

True, it wasn't unusual, but by now, they should have come across *something*.

"What has him in a foul mood?"

Even though Icezak whispered the words, Keirak heard them as if he stood right by him. He didn't stop or respond, just continued swinging his blade through the air as sweat slid down his skin. They would approach a clearing in about a mile, their journey taking them down the same path every time. The meadow was where most of the creatures choose to graze—the tamer ones that is.

He picked up his pace until he was soon jogging through the brush, his fellow warriors trying to keep up and cursing in confusion. He didn't care though, just wanted to get out there and slay something, hoping a little bit of violence would ease some of the rage that burned inside of him.

They made it to the clearing quickly, each taking a post among the thick trees and heavy brush that was scattered around. They might sit there hours, or get lucky and catch something within minutes—he hoped for the latter. He leaned against the thick trunk of a *Peonnta* tree, its smooth black trunk free of any flaws and as soft as the finest fabrics. He set his sword in his lap—his body coiled tight, his eyes scanning every inch of his surroundings.

Hour after hour past and, finally, a large *Borra* beast waddled into the clearing. Its twin trunks too heavy for the creature to hold up, its pink snout running wet as it collected debris from the meadow floor. The beast was well fed, its body plump all over, a feast that would feed all of his tribe. He set his blade on the ground and stood slowly, drawing his sword from his back and taking a step forward. The creature was unaware of what was about to happen. Its face was buried in the ground as it grunted and growled. He looked at each of his brethren, their big bodies hidden but still visible to his superior sight. He didn't need to speak to let them know this was his kill. He waited until each nodded their heads and then he leaped into the clearing, sword drawn high, war cry spilling from his throat.

Chapter Eight

Keirak and the other warriors headed back home, two short days away, their bodies packing various supplies and numerous animal carcasses. They planned on stopping at one more tribe before they returned home, a small tribe known as the *Klaukka* tribe. They were known for their medicinal herbs that no other tribe could re-create. They were fiercer than the *Monna He*, the males more physically powerful, but friendly and always welcoming. They always stopped at their tribe last since the herbs they gathered from the *Klaukka's* needed to stay cold.

"I wish we were already there. I don't know why I got stuck carrying the *borra* beast."

Keirak, and the other two warriors ignored Icezak grumbling.

"I just don't see why I am carrying the heaviest carcass. Keirak was the one who killed the damn thing."

"Shut up already. We are all carrying our fair share. We are close to the *Klaukka* tribe and you can rest yourself then."

Demariak's words were low and annoyed, and Keirak smiled despite his current mood. True, he was anxiously awaiting his arrival back to the mountain, to his love, but he didn't know how he could keep his indiscretion from her. He wanted to tell her, but he was ashamed with himself.

"I can see the smoke about a half mile ahead, we can get something to eat and rest there for the night." Demariak stood at the front of their group, the huge carcass slung across his shoulders, gray blood dripping on the jungle floor.

They finally made it to the large village, the leader of the tribe, Trayk, seated in a stone thrown atop a podium. His queen sat beside him, her dark hair and pale skin common of their kind.

"Ah, you have returned. I am most pleased to see you, my friends."

Even though Trayk acted as though he was surprised by their arrival, Keirak knew better. The *Klaukka* warriors were stationed around the perimeter of the village, hidden so cleverly not even he could spot them. Demariak dropped the carcass on the ground and walked toward the other leader. Trayk walked down the podium with a wide smile on his face and stopped in front of Demariak. They gripped forearms, as warriors do in welcome, and slapped each other on the back. They spoke softly to each other, Keirak and the other ZorZacks setting their supplies down and waiting for word on the next course of action.

Demariak motioned for them to follow as they made their way toward Trayk's private chamber. They walked into a modest sized hut and toward two small wooden doors bolted to the ground. Trayk lifted one side, the four of them following him down a set of stone stairs that lead to the *Klaukka* leader's private quarters. It was a large room, carved right out of the earth—candles already lit and showcasing exquisite furniture as well as a wall full of weapons. A circular table sat in the center of the room, twelve seats stationed around it with a large candlelit chandelier hanging above its center.

"Please, have a seat." He gestured toward the chairs and sat down. "I am most pleased you have chosen to visit our village. It has been too long since I have seen the great ZorZack warriors." He clapped his hands, a female seeming to appear out of nowhere, a large tray in her hands. She set the tray on the table, distributed large mugs and set a jug in the center of the table. "Thank you, Maheena, you may leave us." He picked up the jug and poured bright red liquid into each of their mugs, a serious look covering his features. "Have you heard the news?"

Keirak took a sip of the sweet liquid, the concoction a popular drink amongst this particular tribe. It wasn't his place to address the leader of the tribe, so he sat back, sipped on his drink, and waited for Demariak to respond.

"We have not. We have been on our journey and have not heard any news. Please, tell us what you have learned."

"I fear it is not pleasant news." Trayk shook his head and took a sip of his drink. "It seems there have been some reports of a rogue tribe that has slaughtered several villages across the *Zella* Sea."

Keirak's heart stopped at what he heard. His past flashed before him in rapid succession, the deaths of his people playing over and over again in his mind. "What have you heard?" Everyone turned to stare at him, surprised he spoke when two leaders were conversing. He didn't care—his worst fears had manifested themselves right before his eyes. It could all be a coincidence, but he had a feeling in the pit of his gut that said otherwise. "What of this tribe? What did they look like?" The scarred face of his mother's murderer was ingrained in his brain, a picture he would never forget.

"Well, I have not heard much, but what I have is not pleasant. I hear they are ruthless in their pursuits. They are cruel and cold, very calculating in their hunts. The only physical description I have heard is about the leader—the scarred one as they have called him."

Keirak gripped his mug tightly, knowing without a doubt this was the same tribe that ransacked his village.

"What is it?"

Demariak's deep voice penetrated the anger that coursed through his body. "I fear this is a lot worse than anyone realizes."

"Care to elaborate?" Trayk's voice was filled with confusion.

Keirak watched with dread as Demariak ran a hand through his short hair and breathed out. "We have heard of this tribe, they have no name, but their reputation is devious."

"Why have I never heard of them before now?" Trayk asked as he set his mug down.

Keirak shrugged and spoke up. "Their last attack in this area was long ago. After that, they seemed to disappear. I suspect they keep moving, possibly traveling great distance so that they are not caught."

"Well, they will not get very far with us. Our warriors are highly trained."

Everyone nodded, agreeing with Trayk, but Keirak knew better. His tribe had been highly trained, the *KayKow* warriors ruthless in their hunt, fierce males that had defeated many. They were no more though, all because of a rouge tribe that extinguished them.

"If they are smart they will not come across the *Zella* Sea. We have many allies on this land and will fight to the death."

Keirak had no doubt that was exactly how it would end, whether it be the rogues or their own, there would be plenty of blood spilled.

"Father?"

Everyone turned to see a small female at the foot of the stairs.

"Ah, my precious, Kalina, come here my daughter and say hello to the great ZorZack warriors."

They all stood—a tradition they did when a high ranking individual entered a room. She was Trayk's daughter, only eighteen, but had many suitors lined up to mate her. She was very slender with the same black flowing hair and pale blue eyes as her mother and father.

"Great warriors." she bowed her head, a form of respect for a visiting warrior. "I will come back, I had no idea you were meeting with my father."

"It is okay, daughter. What do you inquire about?"

She hesitated a moment and continued. "I would like to ask permission to go to the creek. I would like to pick the berries that grow there to make pies tonight."

Keirak glanced away and took a sip of his drink, noticing in the corner of his eye how Icezak's undivided attention was on her. He glanced sideways, lust clear on his fellow warriors face. Keirak chuckled softly, knowing that would be something Icezak would never attain. Of course, that was what appealed to Icezak so much, the fact that he could not have what he desired.

"I can only allow you to go if you can find one of the males to escort you. There are new dangers that present themselves, and it is no longer safe for you to be alone, even if it is just a short distance."

She didn't argue, just nodded her head and turned to leave.

"I will escort her to pick the berries with your permission." Everyone turned, shocked as Icezak stood and addressed Trayk. "I will see to it that she is safe."

Keirak looked at Trayk, his eyes narrowed as he watched Icezak with fatherly concern.

"If it is okay with Kalina, I do not see any problem with you escorting her. I have no doubts a fierce warrior like yourself could protect her."

Icezak nodded and then looked down at himself, realizing he, like the other warriors, was covered in dirt and sweat. "I must clean first."

It was a sight, something Keirak thought he would never see in his existence—Icezak actually wanting to appear clean for a female. On a normal day, Icezak could care less about his appearance. As long as he found a willing female—which he always did—he didn't care how dirty he was. Keirak couldn't help but chuckle as Icezak stumbled out of the chamber, his eyes trained on Kalina the entire time.

Chapter Nine

Kitty stood at the main entrance of the cave, her heart pounding quickly, her palms sweaty from nervousness. Today was the day Keirak and the other warriors would return. She brought her hand to her mouth and started to bite at her nails. It was a dirty habit, but because she was so antsy about seeing him again, she couldn't help it. True, it had only been a couple of weeks, but those two weeks seemed like ages.

Mena stood a few feet down from her, baby Nea in her arms and a lost look on her face. She still didn't look the best, her skin much too pale, but Mena assured her she was fine. She turned her attention back to the cave, the females all around her talking anxiously about the warriors return. Almost all of the tribe was stationed here, waiting for their return and ready to welcome them with open arms. A young boy came running from the mouth of the cave, a big smile on his face as he shouted in the ZorZack language. She could understand only a few words, but understood enough that he told everyone the warriors were back. She breathed out deeply and craned her neck to see if she could catch a glimpse of them.

The first warrior to enter the cave was Demariak, his face grim and dirty as he carried the carcass of a creature she couldn't quite distinguish. He dropped everything he carried on the ground, Mena rushing over to him, oblivious to the dirt that covered his body. The next to enter was Icezak who did the same with the things he carried. Several women rushed toward him, cooing and gasping over his cuts and bruises.

She kept watch at the entrance, spotting Draydon coming through but not seeing Keirak. She walked a little bit into the tunnel, her hands twisting together as she wondered where he was. She turned around and looked at everyone greeting the returned warriors, their smiles bright enough to light up the entire cave. When she turned back around she gasped and stepped back as she looked right into Keirak's face. Dirt covered him as he carried another strange looking creature. "Keirak." His name was a whisper on her lips, but she knew he heard her nonetheless.

"Hello, *fallina*." He smiled, but it didn't quite reach his eyes.

She stared at him with an open mouth as he walked right past her, dumped his belongings on the ground, and kept going. She stood there frozen, not knowing what just happened as she watched the empty space Keirak had just occupied. She rushed to follow him, needing to see him—needing to talk to him. She rounded the corner, seeing his big body walking quickly toward the hot springs. She knew he could hear her footsteps but he didn't stop, didn't even slow down.

Her heart felt tight in her chest as she ran to keep up with his long strides. *What's wrong with him?* She saw his fleeting shape enter the hot spring cave and picked up her pace. Once she entered the cavern, she spotted him at one of the far corners. Her eyes grew wide as he slipped off his ripped and dirty leathers and slipped into the water. She got a quick glance of the tattoo that covered his hips and ran down his thighs before he went into the water. The dark ink resembled flames, the color twisting and curving around his golden skin.

She took a few steps closer to him and tentatively called his name, "Keirak?" He went under the water and came up on the other side of the hot springs so that he now faced her. Water dripped from his blond hair and down his rippled chest, his green eyes staring right at her as if he didn't even know who she was. "Hi. I missed you." She didn't know what to say, didn't even know if she should have followed him. He acted like he wanted nothing to do with her.

"I missed you, too."

His voice didn't hold the same kind of emotion it had before he left, and she wondered what had happened during his journey that would make him act like this. "Did you? Your actions are speaking differently."

"I'm just tired, Kitty."

Kitty, not *fallina*. There was something definitely different about him. "Is everything okay? I mean, you're acting very differently." He didn't speak for the longest time, just stared at her with an almost pained expression that worried her. "It's all right. We can talk later." She didn't wait for a response, just turned and left. Before she stepped a foot outside the chamber, he was there, his powerful presence clear even though her back was to him. She turned around, his chest taking up her view, the droplets of water sliding down his smooth chest and splashing to the ground.

"I'm sorry."

His face looked haunted, his features distant as he stared down at her and cupped her cheek. She leaned her head into his embrace, closing her eyes and letting his warmth seep into her. "Please, kiss me." She stood on her toes and ran her lips against his. His body was tense, his eyes closed as he breathed in deeply. Her kiss was gentle, the lightest of kisses that teased more than anything. His hand gripped the back of her head, bringing her closer so that their lips meshed together as one. She wrapped her arms around his massive shoulders, not caring that her clothing was becoming wet, just needing to be as close to him as possible. His hands slid down to her waist, pulling her hips forward so that his erection pressed against her core.

He broke the kiss and rested his forehead against hers. "I missed you so much."

"I missed you, too." She brought his mouth back to hers, running her tongue along the seam of his lips and urging him to open for her. Their mouths fused together, their tongues swirling and dancing and igniting her arousal to a boiling point. His hands landed on her ass, lifting her up so that she was forced to wrap her legs around his waist for balance. She gripped his shoulders tighter, their mouths never breaking as he started to walk.

Her eyes stayed closed as they kissed, his erection moving against her body with every step he took. She moaned into his mouth, running her hands in his hair and gripping the wet strands as she tilted her head and deepened the kiss. She was vaguely aware of a door opening and closing, and in the next instant she was lying on her back, Keirak above her, his face mere inches from her own.

"Take it off, *fallina*." He pulled back, his cock straining forward as he stood at the edge of the bed.

She looked around quickly, taking in the barren room that was void of anything except the bed she lay on. She swallowed and looked back at him, his face a mask of pure lust, his eyes half mast as they roamed across her body. She shivered at the intensity of that one look and slid toward the edge of the bed. This is what she wanted, what she had been waiting for since he left. He took a few more steps backward, his eyes never leaving hers. She slowly stood and smoothed her hands down her dress, her heart beating quickly as her nerves took over. She dipped her eyes down to his cock, the head an angry red and clear fluid seeping from the tip. She swallowed at his size, his girth and length enough to make any woman a little nervous.

"Take it off."

He spoke low but his voice held a dominance that told her she needed to do just as he said…she loved it. She looked at his body again, all power and male masculinity that made her wet with lust. The tattoo added to the allure, added to the powerful aura that encased his being. She moved her hand to her shoulder and slowly slipped off the first sleeve, her eyes never leaving his. She did the same to the other shoulder, her breathing picking up as the fabric slid down and pooled at her feet. She wore nothing underneath, and she was fully aware of the way Keirak's eyes ran the length of her body.

"You are so beautiful, you take my breath away."

She swallowed as he stepped forward, her body so sensitive with arousal the very air seemed to tease her nerve endings. His presence was so powerful that it made her feel faint and light-headed. She placed her hands on his chest, the smooth skin beneath her hands hot to the touch. All she wanted was to feel Keirak's hard body covering hers, and feel his firm lips caressing her own. She wanted him, needed him, and had to have him now.

"I did things on the journey, Kitty, things that I am not proud of."

She leaned up and stopped his words with a kiss, her tongue slipping inside the hot recess of his mouth and stroking every inch she could. She didn't want him to relive the horrors of his trip, didn't want him to have to remember the kills he no doubt spoke of. She just wanted to make him feel as hot and needy as she was, wanted him to forget and just *feel*. They moved as one to the bed, his body once again covering hers as they fell onto it.

He rolled onto his back, taking her with him so that she straddled his hips. They continued to kiss, their mouths working together, their tongues moving against each other in an erotic dance. His hands smoothed down her back, just barley skimming the top of her ass before moving back up. He teased and tantalized her, brought her arousal so high she shook from it. She broke the kiss and looked down at him, feeling his rock hard erection pressing against her slit and wanting nothing more than to let it slide inside of her.

"There's something I should tell you." She would be lying if she said she wasn't a little scared. She didn't know how he would react to the knowledge that she was a virgin and horribly inexperienced. Would he even fit? She wasn't naive, she knew there would be some pain, but wasn't it natural to worry about that? She looked down at him, his eyes full of love as he ran his fingers down her cheek and outlined her lips.

"We don't have to do this right now. We have all the time in the world, *fallina*."

She ran her hand through his platinum blond hair, the strands so soft they felt like silk. *He thinks you don't want to do this.* She couldn't help but smile at his comment, the complete opposite of what she really wanted. "I want this to happen, it's just that, well…I've never done this before." The last part was softer than the rest and she looked away, her cheeks becoming hot as embarrassment coursed through her. She felt his finger run under her chin and bring her face back forward. He didn't say anything, just watched her.

"I don't want to hurt you, *fallina*." His words were whispered as he stared at her mouth.

"I want this, Keirak, so bad." He groaned and brought her face down to his, brushing his lips across her forehead before rolling them over again until his body covered hers. His lips ran down her cheek and over her nose, finally resting against her lips. His tongue gently ran across hers until she opened and let him in. His hips started a slow thrust against hers, his erection sliding through her slit and bumping her clit. His hands caressed each of her breasts, his thumbs tweaking at the nipples until they stood stiff and hard. He moved his lips down her jaw, over her collarbone and finally covered one of her engorged nipples. His mouth was hot and wet, his tongue swirling around the stiff peak and driving her crazy. With every lap of his tongue, and thrust of his hips, lightning shot through her clit until she was thrashing her head against the pillows.

He pulled away from her nipple, the resounding pop moving through her like an aphrodisiac to all of her senses. He slid down her body, and she opened her eyes to watch his descent. His eyes stayed on her face as he placed his hands on the inside of her thighs, spreading them wide. Her breathing was ragged, her heart beating quickly as his tongue peeked out and touched her clit. The act was so soft and gentle, but so powerful it rocked her to the core and had her arching her hips. His hands moved inward, his thumbs slowly pulling her labia apart until she was completely exposed.

She shifted, a little uncomfortable, as his eyes continued to watch her. His head moved in, his tongue licking her clit and then sliding down her slit to plunge into her hole. She gasped and threw her head back, her hands gathering the fabric on the bed and gripping it tight. "Oh. My. God." The pleasure he caused was incredible, his mouth so hot and wet it had her womb clenching and her juices spilling out. His thumb worked on her clit as his tongue stabbed into her vagina, mimicking an act she knew was about to come. Her climax was seconds away, just a couple more flicks of his thumb, a couple more probes of his tongue, and it would wash through her. She arched her back, her nipples drawing up tight as her orgasm exploded inside of her and had her whole body going rigid. She moaned loud and long, not able to control herself as she thrusted her hips into Keirak's face. He wrung out her climax until she was panting and weak.

Chapter Ten

She slowly opened her eyes and looked down, feeling Keirak's hands clenching and unclenching at her thighs. She ran her hand over his and smiled, so completely sated it was hard to keep her eyes open. He moved up her body, his muscles flexing and bunching as he braced his arms on either side of her head.

"I love you, *fallina*." His mouth claimed hers, his cock probing at her entrance, the head hot and hard as steel.

"You never did tell me what that means." He smiled down at her and kissed her forehead.

"It means, 'my beautiful flower.'"

She leaned up and kissed him, her hands framing his cheeks as she felt his hand move between their bodies. He placed the hot head of his cock against her entrance and she gasped.

"I have wanted this for so long. I will be so good to you, Kitty, so gentle." His mouth trailed kisses over her face as he slowly pushed into her.

She gasped as the head slipped inside, his eyes on her face, his expression full of love. "I know you will." And she did, with every part of her being, she knew he would be a gentle lover. She whispered the words, her eyes wide as he pushed another inch into her. It burned and there was pain, but the farther he slipped in, the warmer her body grew—the more pleasure he caused her. She could feel every hard ridge and line that made up his huge cock. She closed her eyes, the pain mixing with a pleasure so powerful it took her breath away.

He suddenly stopped, and she opened her eyes to look at him. She swallowed at the intense expression that covered his face. He closed his eyes. Sweat beaded on his brow as he reared back slightly. She knew what was coming, and she willed herself to relax. He pushed forward, breaking through her innocence—her gasping as he groaned. He didn't move once he was fully buried inside of her, just framed her face with his hands and gently kissed her.

"I'm sorry, I know it hurt."

Her vagina clenched around his cock, and they both sucked in air. He was so big and thick it felt as if he filled every inch of her. "That wasn't too bad." It was a lie. It did hurt, and it was uncomfortable, but as he stared down at her, his green eyes filled with so much love that it broke her heart, she knew it was all worth it. "I love you." She whispered the words, needing to say them to him, needing to say it while they made love.

"I love you, too, *fallina*." He slowly pulled out, and she opened her mouth in a silent cry as pleasure shot through her. She could feel her body growing wetter, coating him and making him slide easily from her. He stopped at her entrance, poised there for a moment before slowly pushing back in. He groaned long and deep, his own pleasure evident on his face.

"If you could only know how alive you make me feel."

His hips picked up a faster rhythm, his hand moving down her side and over her hip to grip her thigh. He lifted it, wrapping it around his waist and doing the same to the other one. This new angle had her moaning, the penetration seeming deeper as she became lost in pleasure. His hips moved in and out of her, the sound of soaked sex slapping together so erotic she felt her climax approaching rapidly. "I'm so close." She couldn't help the words that spilled from her mouth, didn't even care as her body lit up so brightly it blinded her.

She clenched around his cock so tightly the pain mixed with pleasure and caused an exquisite burn to travel through her. She gripped his shoulders, her nails digging into his skin as her orgasm crested over and over again, a never ending tidal wave of pleasure. His hips didn't ease their thrusting as he continued to pound into her with such fervor she thought she would pass out. He tensed above her, his groan loud as they stared at each other, sweat coating their bodies, their breathing erratic. She felt the hot jets of his semen coat her insides, the sensation enough to cause another orgasm to ripple through her.

He collapsed above her, his body big and heavy, but welcome nonetheless. His hands smoothed across her overheated flesh as he whispered to her in his language. He rolled off of her, pulling her close so that she felt wrapped in a blanket of protectiveness and love. She closed her eyes, a smile on her face as she let sleep claim her.

* * * *

Kitty slowly opened her eyes, the room having a soft glow around the edges as she turned to her side. She was sore in the most delicious places, and smiled as she thought of what Keirak and she had done. He faced her, his eyes closed, his breathing deep and even. The sheet pooled low on his hips, the dark ink of his tattoo peeking through the material and tempting her. She ran her hand over one of the flames, his skin so smooth and warm that his heat seeped into her body.

She could see the stiff outline of his erection pressing against the sheet. She swallowed. She looked into his face, her breath catching as he stared at her. He smiled slow and sensual, the kind of smile that made her immediately wet. She didn't move as he pushed himself up and leaned on his elbow, his lips skimming across hers in the sweetest of caresses.

"Let's bathe."

It wasn't a question, but she wouldn't have said no anyway. He slid off the bed, holding his hand out for her as her eyes roamed over his naked form. She slipped her hand into his and let him lead her to the alcove with the ever-present waterfall. He wrapped his arms around her waist and moved them under the warm spray, the water trailing between their bodies and slipping into her already soaked pussy.

"I want you again, but if you're too sore, I understand."

She was sore, but the very thought of him pushing that massive cock into her overshadowed the slight discomfort she felt. She didn't answer him, just leaned back against the smooth rock and slid her leg up his. His eyes dropped down to her exposed cleft, and he growled low in his throat. The water coated her in a sensual slickness that heightened her senses and made her arousal spark and flicker.

His hands slid along her slick skin and gripped her breasts, his head dropping to take a stiff nipple into his mouth and rolling it around his tongue. She breathed out heavily, biting the inside of her cheek as every nip from his teeth shot straight to her clit. Before he got too involved and had her mind going completely blank, she pushed at his chest and sank to her knees. She looked up at him, a smile on her lips as the water beat a steady rhythm across her back.

She dropped her eyes to his cock and licked her lips. She wrapped her hand around his hot flesh as she moved her other hand to cup the heavy sack that lay beneath. A pearl sized drop of fluid seeped from slit at the tip and she swiped her tongue across it, loving the slightly salty and purely male taste of his cum. She sucked the head into her mouth, moving her lips around the thick crown and tasting his salty essence slip across her tongue. She closed her eyes and moaned, feeling Keirak's hand slide along her head and grip a chunk of her hair as his hips pushed forward.

She moved his balls around in her hand, the heavy weight a welcoming feeling as she tried to take as much of him in her mouth as she could. She couldn't even take half of him so she worked with what she could get, needing him to feel the same pleasure she felt. She bobbed her head, her tongue touching all around his shaft, her teeth ever so gently scrapping on every down stroke.

He groaned and moaned above her, his words roughened and low as he spoke in his native tongue. She moved her head up and down quicker, wanting to feel his cum fill her mouth and slide down her throat. She rolled his balls in her hand, matching the rhythm her mouth made, moaning around the head of his cock and feeling him stiffen. He tried to pull away. She let go of his balls, gripped his ass with both hands, and pulled his hips forward.

"*Fallina*, you must stop."

She moaned again and picked up her pace, his hips thrusting forward as she tasted the first pulse of his seed shoot into her mouth. He groaned loud and long above her. Jet after jet of his hot semen slid down her throat, the taste so addicting she knew she would never get enough. When she felt that last pulse of cum shoot out of him, she sucked on the tip, her tongue sliding along the slit and cleaning all the evidence of his orgasm away. The head came out of her mouth with a resounding pop, and she leaned back and stared up at him.

He looked down at her, awe and shock covering his features as he breathed. His cock was still hard as rock, the head still an angry color of red. He picked her up off the ground, his lips claiming hers as his tongue stabbed into her mouth. He was wild and untamed, pushing her against the wall of the alcove and gripping her ass tightly. He pulled her up so she had no other option but to wrap her legs around his waist. He slid his cock inside of her so forcefully they both groaned in unison.

"You're so tight and hot. I have never felt anything as good as you wrapped around my cock."

His hips pounded into her fast and hard, so uninhibited she screamed from the intensity of it. He turned them around so he leaned against the wall, his thrust into her unrelentingly and she tilted her head back and screamed out her release. It washed through her, so wild and so forceful, she saw stars.

Even after her climax eased into a pleasure filled burn, he continued to move his hips in her, his body tensing as his cock seemed to grow bigger, longer, until his semen shot into her womb. Her vagina clenched around him, milking his cock for every last drop until he sagged against the wall, cradling her head against her chest and kissing her head.

"I love you."

His words were soft against her hair and brought tears of happiness to her eyes. This is where she wanted to be, where she needed to be, now and forever. "I love you, too."

Chapter Eleven

Icezak sat at the large stone table, platters of food laid out before him like a feast, but his appetite was lacking. He couldn't get his mind off Kalina, the tiny female that he had escorted to pick berries. He could remember the time he spent with her so clearly, so vividly.

He cleaned himself up quickly, not wanting the dirt and blood from his journey to taint her innocence. She met him at the edge of the jungle, her white gown formed to perfection against her tiny body and showing him her glorious assets. He had never felt this kind of attraction before—never the kind that stole his breath and made all rational thought escape his brain.

Her black hair shone under the rays of the sun like polished obsidian, tempting him but reminding him she was far too perfect for a warrior like him to touch. She was a forbidden prize, something he knew he would never be able to acquire, but teasing him nonetheless. She led the way, his eyes having a hard time looking anywhere but at the way her ass swayed as she moved.

"Do you like the tuka *berries?"*

She looked over her shoulder, dark eyelashes framing light blue eyes and spearing him in the chest. Her voice was the softest and sweetest he had ever heard, and he ached to hear more. He swallowed and shook his head, not trusting himself to speak, thankful when she smiled and turned around. A creek greeted them and she walked toward the bright blue water and bent. Her dress rode up, showing him an enticing view of her creamy pale legs.

He scanned their surroundings, knowing he should be keeping a diligent eye on the jungle and less on her body. He couldn't help himself though, and time and time again, he found his eyes drawn to her. She scooped up a handful of water and brought it to her mouth, taking a long drink and making his cock grow painfully hard. He watched a trail of water slide down her chin and disappear into her dress. His erection jerked in appreciation. He quickly adjusted himself, not about to let a female as young as her see the evidence of his arousal. She may be considered an adult, but the fact that she was only eighteen made him keep his distance.

She stood and smoothed her tiny hands down her gown, walking over to group of white bushes with bright green berries. She didn't bring a basket and he wondered how she planned on carrying the berries she picked, but that thought soon left his brain when he saw her lift her dress. She gripped the edge of her gown so that it made a makeshift basket and started to pick the berries and toss them in. The dress was to her knees, and so when she pulled it up, it offered him the most delectable view of her thighs. He turned around, continuing to scan the area as he attempted to get himself under control. His cock pulsed in his leathers, and he clenched his teeth as he heard her light footsteps approach. He turned around, fists clenched, and breathing deeply as he forced a smile.

"I can't believe you have never tasted a tuka berry. They are most delicious."

He turned around, surprised to see her mere inches from him. He watched the scene in slow motion, his heart picking up a fast rhythm as his breathing became shallower. She picked a berry from her dress, her hand bringing it slowly toward him as a gentle smile covered her bow like lips.

He took an involuntary step back, her movements following his until the tips of her fingers grazed his lips. She was poised on her toes, berry in hand as she pressed it into his mouth. The juice slipped across his lips and he opened his mouth, their eyes locked together. He didn't miss how her breathing had changed or how her heart sped up. He could smell her arousal as it peaked, and could see the confusion it created within her. She took several steps back, her hands gripping the hem of her dress as she turned around and breathed out deeply.

"I'm ready to go, please."

It was evident that fear assaulted her at what she felt, and as much as he wanted to reassure he it was natural—normal—he kept his mouth shut and said, "Okay." She walked quickly back to her village, looking over her shoulder several times with brows drawn in confusion.

He hadn't seen her again after that, not even as her tribe gathered to give them a blessing for their journey back home. He didn't know if he should feel happy or offended by her absence. If he had gotten to her that deeply, then he could smile and feel content that she felt the same as he did—felt that same bone shattering connection he felt, but if she disliked what he brought out in her, then that was an entirely different situation, one he didn't even want to dwell on.

* * * *

Kitty lay on her back, her breathing fast, her body covered in sweat. She kicked the sheet off her overheated body and turned to look at Keirak who was in the same state. They had just finished having wild sex, and the pleasure still pulsed through her. His eyes were closed, but she knew he wasn't asleep. Her gaze dropped to the tattoos that twirled around both of his thighs and up to his hips, the dark ink a turn on all in itself. "What does it mean?" She ran her hand along his smooth skin, over the ink, and resting it on his hard, rippled belly. He cracked an eye open and looked over at her, a hard expression instantly masking the after sex glow he had. "Sorry, I didn't mean to pry." She turned on her back, embarrassed by his reaction."

"It just brings up bad memories. Didn't I tell you to never apologize to me?"

His voice was low, yet caring, and she rolled onto her side again to stare at him. He did the same, both of them just watching each other, a comfortable silence surrounding them.

"My birth tribe was known as the *KayKows*. When I was a fledgling, rogues ambushed and slaughtered my people. They took the younger females and children with them, killing all of the older ones, including my mother, and all of the males."

Kitty put her hand on his shoulder, his voice growing distant and sad, and his face taking on that same state. He stared at her, but she could see he really wasn't, his mind was far away reliving his past. "I'm so sorry."

He chuckled humorlessly, sorrow filling it as he lay on his back and put his hands behind his head. "They spared me though, the only male from my tribe to survive—that I know of at least. At first, I tried hunting them down, but it was no use. I was only a boy, and they were experienced hunters and trackers. I went from tribe to tribe, lucky that they took pity and fed and clothed me. This one tribe specialized in body art, and so I had them give me this." He pointed to his tattoos. "It is a vengeance marking, one that will let all others know I have a score to settle.

"Do you ever regret getting it?"

He shook his head, determination on his face. "It makes my memories of my family strong within me. It makes me never forget that day when everything and everyone I loved was taken from me." He breathed out deeply, his eyes flickering toward her. "Not too long after that, the ZorZacks found me and took me in—treated me like one of their own."

She ran her fingers along his square jaw, tears filling her eyes at his words. She could imagine him as a young boy, terrified and hurt, trying to take down an enemy that was so much stronger. She wanted to comfort him, to tell him how much she cared for him, but where did she begin? "Keirak, I can't even begin to tell you how sorry I am. Your loss is so great, but I'm here for you." She made him turn his head so that they stared at each other. "*I'm really here for you*, for anything you need. I love you so much. You are such a strong and caring man, a warrior your tribe would have been proud of." As they looked at each other, she wanted to let him she knew how he felt. She knew all about losing what you held so dear. She took a deep breath, about to tell him what only a select few knew. "My family is also dead, killed right in front of me when I was young."

His hand scooped hers up and brought it to his lips for a soft kiss, "I'm so sorry, *fallina*." In just that instant, his trouble was pushed to the side as he looked at her with love.

Tears fell from her eyes and slid down her cheek. "When I was ten, my family went on vacation to this cabin in the mountains. We used to go there every summer—it was so beautiful and quiet, so peaceful." She wiped the tears from her eyes and sniffed, her memories flooding back to her at a fast pace. "My brother was five years older than I was and would always tease me about monsters in the woods. I believed him, and so one night those monsters really did come out of the forest. Three masked men invaded our house, killing my whole family."

She closed her eyes as those vivid images crashed through her. "I watched everything from the upstairs—watched those violent things they did right through the banister. I was young, but I knew they would check the house for other people, so I hid. There was a crawl space in my closet, hidden so well it was virtually invisible. I hid in there as I heard them go through my room." She stared at the ceiling, her tears slipping down the sides of her face. "So you see, I know how you feel, losing the ones you love. I got on with my life, met Mena and we became best friends. She's like a sister to me, her own loss of family bringing us close together." She felt the bed shift as he came closer to her.

"My little *fallina*, please don't cry."

He brought her close to his warmth and wrapped his arms around her, all of his love seeping right into her and making her smile despite her sadness. "We're two peas in the same pod, two souls that are meant for each other." She looked over at him, believing what she spoke with such conviction she hoped he believed it, too. They both had a great loss, such a great tragedy that they belonged together—to pick up the pieces and start anew. She ran her finger over Keirak's cheekbone, down his jaw line, and around his lips. She felt different with him, felt warmer and not so alone. He made that emptiness that she had been carrying around inside of her seem bearable.

He held her for hours, whispering soft words in his language that she knew were meant to smooth. She cried into his chest, but she didn't care, he just continued to hold her and stoke her hair. That's how she fell asleep, wrapped in Keirak's warm embrace, feeling that hollow ache disappear for the first time in years.

* * * *

Kitty walked with Keirak to the dining chamber, their hands intertwined, warmth encompassing her. A week had passed since they both opened up and shared their horrid pasts. She felt closer to him—the bond that they built together seeming unbreakable now.

They entered the dining chamber, everyone gathered in a large circle, their voices raised with excitement. She looked at Keirak, confusion clear on his face as well. They walked to the group of people, overhearing a male talk about the birth of the future leader. She felt her eyes widen, and she ran out the door toward Mena's room. She could feel Keirak behind her, his presence strong as he followed.

It didn't sound like there were any complications from the happy expressions of the tribe members faces, but she knew how Mena looked just a few days ago, and it worried her. She rounded the last corner and stopped in front of Mena and Demariak's door, her breathing fast and heavy as she gave a quick rap on the wood. She heard a muffled voice, not understanding what they said but bursting through anyway. Mena lay in her massive bed, silk pillows all around her as Nea sat on her father's lap.

"Are you okay?" Kitty stepped forward and stopped when she saw the small bundle in Mena's arms. She covered her mouth in shock, tears of happiness stinging her eyes as she took a few more steps forward.

"I'm fine. Did you run over here?"

Kitty nodded, not trusting her voice as she stared down at the tiny baby wrapped in a white blanket.

"His name is Cayllum."

"Why didn't you tell me?" Kitty sat at the edge of the bed, Nea climbing off her father's lap and crawling over to her. "Hi, precious, you're a big sissy now."

"KiKi."

The little girl's voice speared through Kitty, finally being the finishing touch that had her tears falling down her cheeks. "You said my name. What a smart little girl you are."

"I didn't tell anyone yet." Mena's eyes narrowed and she glared at her husband. "You told everyone already?" A sheepish look crossed his features. "I'm sorry, I just couldn't help myself. I went to Kitty's room to tell her, but she wasn't there."

Kitty looked down, her face burning because she knew why she wasn't in her room—she was with Keirak. She kissed Nea on the head and looked over at the newest baby.

"Want to hold him?"

Kitty nodded, setting Nea on the bed and taking the small bundle. She cradled him in her arms, the baby fussing slightly and then opening his big, dove gray eyes. "He has your eyes, Mena." She looked up and smiled, the love she felt for them so strong. She looked over at Keirak who stood by the door, his focus on her and a strange expression covering his features.

"I would like to offer my congratulations to you and yours. May health and safety forever be with you." Demariak got up and walked toward Keirak, the two of them gripping forearms before embracing and smacking each other on the back.

"Is this why you weren't feeling good?"

"I don't know, maybe. He was a big baby so maybe that had something to do with it. Or maybe I just ate bad beans." They both laughed softly.

She handed Cayllum back to Mena and said goodbye, knowing she needed her rest and would want to be alone with Demariak and Nea. As the door shut behind them, she looked at Keirak, love and longing reflected in his eyes.

"As I watched you hold that child, it just looked so right. It is an image I will never forget—so beautiful and innocent. It becomes you."

She stared at Keirak shocked, the words he just spoke so gentle and loving, it brought more tears to her eyes. She stepped up to him and wrapped her arms around his waist, resting her head on his chest and closing her eyes. "*You* feel so right to me. I love you." The embrace was nothing sexual, just the two of them holding each other and letting their love surround them. It was a perfect moment, a moment that was interrupted by female screams.

Chapter Twelve

Kitty looked up at Keirak and gasped when he pushed her back, stepping in front of her as Demariak busted through his bedroom door, slamming it shut behind him and racing down the hallway.

"I want you to go wait with Mena, under no circumstance do you leave that room." He brought his lips down for a fierce kiss and pushed her through the door.

She stared at Mena whose eyes were wide and who held her two children close to her. "I have to see what's going on." Mena shook her head fast, squeezing Nea close until the little girl started to whine. "You stay here and lock the door behind me." She looked at the door and spotted the thick metal latches on the top, middle and bottom of the door. "As soon as I leave I want you to lock it."

"I know you're not going to be stupid enough to go out there."

Mena's voice was incredulous, but Kitty ignored it. "What if there are women and children hurt out there?"

"There are plenty of warriors who can be more help than you can, just stay put. You're going to end up getting in the way, probably getting hurt and maybe getting others hurt."

Kitty knew Mena was right but she shook her head as she opened the door slightly and peaked around the corner. "I mean it, Mena. Shut this door as soon as I leave." She turned back around, seeing the anger and fear in Mena's eyes. She couldn't just sit here when there might be people hurt. She shut the door behind her and stayed on the other side until she heard the latches click in place. She was thankful that Mena listened this one time. She quietly raced down the hallway to where sounds still originated. Her heart pounded in fear.

She stopped just before she rounded the corner, leaning over the side to see three women huddled together, dirt covering their bodies, and their clothing hanging from them in shreds. Warriors stood around them, their voices loud and filled with anger. She brought her eyes to Keirak's massive form, jealousy filling her as a woman clung to him, her bright red hair standing out against her pale skin. Her clothes also hung off of her, showed her curvy body. Kitty could tell the female was crying and hated herself for her petty feelings. It was clear the woman just wanted to be comforted.

She straightened her shoulders and stepped into the cavern, the females looking right at her with confusion in their eyes. The warriors looked over at Kitty, shock covering their faces as they all turned toward Keirak. He looked down at the woman that clung to him and set her to the side, an expression crossing his face that almost looked guilty.

"What are you doing here? I thought I asked you to stay put."

Asked? More like told. She wasn't going to explain herself. She looked over at the women, ignoring Keirak's question and asking her own. "What happened?"

He breathed out, clearly contemplating whether or not to tell her anything. He ran a hand through his short platinum hair. "That rogue tribe that slaughtered my family has resurfaced. According to the females, they ambushed their villages and killed everyone. They were able to escape and headed here."

She looked over at the women again, her mouth hanging open in shock. Two of them were crying, but the other two seemed more calm—the redhead and a small black haired girl.

She walked toward them, hands out in front of her as she smiled. The redhead moved toward the other women, her complete attention still on Keirak. If Kitty didn't know any better she would have assumed there was a history between the two by the way she stared at him with adoring trust in her eyes.

They eyed her with suspicion, the little black haired girl stepping forward and clearly taking the leadership position. "Hello." She didn't know if they would understand her, but it was worth a shot. She extended her hand, said something in a language Kitty didn't understand, and then addressed the warriors.

"She says her name is Kalina and that she comes from the *Klaukka* tribe."

Kitty looked at Keirak who translated, and then looked back at the female when she began speaking again. She pointed off each female, not needing Keirak to translate what were obviously their names.

"Mahenna, Eyessa, Iteena."

Kitty looked over at the last female she named off, the redhead still staring at Keirak, her body language suggesting a closer relationship than Kitty felt comfortable acknowledging. Iteena moved her eyes over Kitty's body and turned away, dismissing her with a flick of her hair. She looked over at Keirak, his face averted down and his jaw tense. There was something definitely wrong with the redhead, something that didn't feel right to her. Kalina started to speak again, but Kitty kept her eyes on Keirak.

"She says they found each other in the jungle, and since she knew we were here, she decided to seek refuge with us."

His words were soft yet clipped, and he acted very out of character. She turned her eyes back to Kalina, nodded her head and extended her hand. "I'm Kitty." She pointed to herself after she said her name, the girl nodding as if she fully understood. ZorZack females rushed in, clothing and baskets in some of their hands, basins of water in others. Kitty stepped out of the way as the females were led away, all of them leaving the cave except Iteena. She walked up to Keirak and wrapped her arms around his waist, her head resting against his chest as she stared at Kitty.

Kitty watched in shock as the redhead stood on her tip toes and kissed Keirak so quickly she wondered if it really happened. She spoke soft words to Keirak as he pushed her away, his own words hard and angry. Iteena looked up at him, a smile on her face as she ran her hand down his chest, not caring in the least when he kept brushing it off. Finally, Iteena left, her hips swaying so hard Kitty wondered if they would become dislocated. She looked back at Keirak, his dark gaze on Iteena. *Oh yes, there was something definitely going on between the two of them.*

"We need to talk, Kitty."

His voice was deep and hard, completely void of all emotion as he walked up to her. He tried to take her hands, but she stepped out of the way and wrapped them around her middle. She didn't say anything as she waited for him to confess whatever dark secret he was about to reveal.

"That was Iteena. Before you came along, I visited her tribe during journeys, and we would be...close."

Yeah, she knew what he meant when he said "close." Well, it wasn't as bad as what she expected. At least whatever they did happened before they had gotten involved. She blew out a breath and smiled at him, feeling stupid for acting so childish. Obviously, the woman still had feelings for him. Keirak's face was still set hard and without a flicker of emotion. Kitty's confidence fell—*there's more.*

"During this last journey we stopped by the *Moona He* tribe and rested for the night. Iteena tried relentlessly to take me to bed, but I told her I had a female waiting for me. By the end of the night, I was drunk and stumbled into my hut. I woke up thinking I dreamed because you straddled me. I touched and kissed her, thinking it was you, but then realized it was not."

She stared at him, not knowing how to feel about what he just said. "So, you did or didn't have sex?"

He shook his head, his hands going in front of him in surrender. "We did not, but what I did isn't excusable by any means. I should have known right away it wasn't you. I was weak and foolish, and I ask for your forgiveness."

Kitty couldn't help the tears that pricked her eyes. She was glad they hadn't had sex, but just picturing Keirak with another woman, touching and kissing her made her physically sick. "You know what gets me about this whole thing? If you just would have been honest with me from the beginning I probably wouldn't have cared, but the fact that you didn't is what breaks my heart. Would you have even told me if she hadn't showed up—no, probably not." She turned to leave, not going to Keirak's room but to her own. She heard him call her, but he was smart enough not to follow. Maybe she should have just forgiven him, but the fact was she felt deceived. If Iteena hadn't shown up, Kitty knew he would have never told her.

Chapter Thirteen

Two days passed, and Kitty successfully avoided any and all contact with Keirak. She headed over to Mena's room, so confused about everything that she just wanted someone to talk to. She hadn't been fully honest with Mena, almost embarrassed as to the reason why she and Keirak weren't speaking.

She stopped in front of Mena's door, lightly knocking on the wood and opening it when she heard two cries. She smiled when she saw Mena sitting on the floor, baby Cayllum in her arms and little Nea holding a wooden block, fat tears streaming down the little girl's face.

"You don't even know how glad I am to see you. Take him, please."

Kitty walked over to Mena and scoped the baby into her arms, his little cries stopping as she rocked him back and forth. She sat in a chair, Nea crawling over to her and pulling at the hem of her dress. Mena stood, stretched her back and picked up Nea, walking over to her crib and lying her gently inside. "Bad day?"

Mena snorted, finished tucking Nea in, and sat on the edge of the bed. "You don't even know the half of it. I'm beat. Is he asleep yet?"

Kitty looked down, Cayllum's big, gray eyes slowly closed as he made little noises. "Almost." Kitty got up, rocked the baby a few more times, and placed him in the hand-sewn bassinet. She walked over to where Mena sat on the bed, sitting down and falling back. Mena did the same a second later, both of their breaths coming out in a sigh.

"So, how are things going?"

Kitty wasn't stupid. She knew Mena already knew something was up between her and Keirak. "They suck."

"Tell me what's going on."

Kitty turned to her side and propped her head on her hand. "You really haven't heard anything?"

"Well, aside from everyone noticing how you have been avoiding Keirak, no."

She breathed out. "Keirak did things with another woman while he was gone."

"Yeah? So what's the problem? If memory serves me right, the last thing I heard was that you two weren't an item." She looked over at Kitty, a smile on her face and an eyebrow arched.

Who was she kidding? Mena, along with everyone else in the tribe could see what was happening between them. "Okay, well, I know you know things have progressed between us from the last time I spoke about it."

Mena laughed softly. "I knew it! Why did you wait so long before you told me?"

Kitty shrugged, not really knowing why she kept it to herself. "I don't really know. I guess I was scared. Scared of how I felt for him, scared of what was growing between us." She shrugged again and sat up.

"Tell me exactly what he did with the other woman?"

Kitty explained what Keirak did. She also told her about how close the two of them had become.

"Huh. Well, I can see why you're pissed, but I think you're being hard on him."

Kitty looked at her with shock. "What? I gave him my virginity, Mena. I think that gives me some room to be pissed at him for doing all kinds of illicit things with another woman."

Mena held her had up and looked over at the children. "Quiet. You'll wake them and then *I'll* be pissed." She turned back with a smile, her words spoken on a teasing note. "That's not what I mean. I would be pissed also if I were in your shoes. What I meant was that everyone can see how much he cares for you. I'm not excusing what he did, but he did tell you. It may not have been as quick as he should have, but eventually he did. I think you should consider how he is taking this whole thing."

Kitty scoffed at Mena and laid back on the bed, her thoughts going to Keirak. She did think about him all the time. She wondered how he was, how he was handling things, if Iteena was wrapping her body around his.

"I know what you're thinking. You have a scowl on your face that speaks a thousand words. He has been avoiding that redhead like the plague."

"How is he anyway? Have you seen or talked to him?" Kitty sat up, her full attention on Mena.

Mena shrugged. "I haven't seen him, but Demariak says he is like a machine. He hardly talks, hardly eats, and trains with the warriors nonstop. Demariak is actually worried about him. I think you should talk to him. I'm not saying forgive him, you do that when you're ready, but just talk to him, talk about this whole situation."

Kitty thought about it, knowing Mena had good points and missing Keirak desperately. She couldn't stay mad at him forever, and as much as the whole situation sucked, what was done was done.

She said goodbye to Mena and closed the door behind her, staring at the rock wall, her emotions were so up in the air that she couldn't even grasp them.

* * * *

Kitty walked into the dining chamber, making her way through the throng of people that ate and talked. She didn't see Keirak, but knew someone in here would know where he was. She saw many of the warriors with naked women on their laps as they fondled their breasts with one hand and ate their food with the other. She walked up to Merak, smiling nervously as he stopped eating and looked up at her. He had a big-breasted brunette on his lap, her nipples pierced and her tongue sliding over his ear. "Sorry to interrupt, but do you know where Keirak is?" The woman paid no attention to Kitty as she continued to rub herself on Merak's bare chest, her hand disappearing beneath the table.

"I have not seen him today, but lately he has been in the training arena. Do you know where that is?"

She nodded, thanking him and quickly leaving before things started really getting pornographic. She remembered where the arena was from when Mena had given me the initial tour. It basically was just a huge cavern with a dirt floor and stone seating built into the walls. It reminded her of something gladiators would train in, at least from what she had seen in the movies. The arena was far into the belly of the mountain, and the farther she descended, the colder the air became.

She rounded the corner and slowly made her way toward the opening of the cavern. Wall sconces were filled with bright, burning candles alongside her, and she stopped right in the entranceway. She stared wide-eyed at the scene in front of her, something that truly did resemble a gladiator fight.

Keirak's back was to her, cuts marring his flesh, blood steadily streaming down his skin and dripping onto the floor. He was fist fighting with Kyros, a warrior that had just returned from a mission. Kyros's black, shoulder-length hair was plastered to his forehead from his sweat, his gold colored eyes seeming to glow in the dimly lit arena like a beacon of light. She watched, her heart beating frantically as they circled each other before slamming into one another, fists flying and grunts ringing out.

Blood sprayed in every direction, and she gasped as Kyros's slammed his fist into Keirak's face. Keirak stumbled back before righting himself and throwing his fist into the side of Kyros's abdomen. Kitty stepped further in, her hands going to her mouth to stifle the cry that welled up in her throat. She didn't dare say anything for fear that it would distract Keirak. In the next instant the fight was over, both of them stumbling back and sagging as they caught their breath. That was when Kyros caught sight of her, his head nodding in her direction as he looked at Keirak.

The next moment happened in slow motion, Keirak turning around, his body and face covered in blood, his eyes widening as he stared at her. She was vaguely aware of Kyro's exiting, leaving Kitty and Keirak alone in the bloodied arena. "Hi." She didn't know what else to say. "Are you okay? Are you really hurt?" Her worry for him overshadowed any kind of anger that she had initially felt.

"They will heal. I'm sorry you have to see me this way."

She watched him walk over to one of the stone tables and grab a cloth. He wiped his face, grabbing the rest of his things before walking toward her and stopping a few feet away. He had a nasty cut above his right eyebrow, the blood still seeping out of it slowly. He had a black eye forming on the left side, along with numerous other cuts and bruises that covered his body. "What happened? Why are you so beat up?"

He shrugged, throwing his animal hide sack over his shoulder, his gaze never leaving hers. "It is a way to make the time pass."

He didn't say anything else, and Kitty could see how much their separation had bothered him also. "Can we go somewhere and talk?" He looked almost surprised by her comment and nodded after a minute. She followed him out of the arena and back to his room.

"Do you mind if I clean up? I smell of blood and sweat."

She shook her head, her heart rate picking up as he quickly took of his leathers and stepped into his bathing chamber. She swallowed, suddenly feeling embarrassed for staring at him when they hadn't spoken to each other in days. He kept her back toward her and she couldn't help but appreciate all of his toned and tanned skin. She turned around and made her way toward the bed, sitting on the edge and keeping her back toward him. Several minutes later, she heard him rustling behind her and she looked over her shoulder.

His back was to her again, a strip of cloth wrapped around his waist as he dried his chest off with another piece. She instantly became wet at the sight. Something about the scene seemed extremely erotic. He turned his head toward her, his bright green stare spearing her and embarrassing her further. She quickly turned around, feeling so childish for how she was acting. "Sorry." She didn't know why she apologized, but it seemed like the right thing to do. He stood in front of her in the next instance and she gasped.

"What would you like to talk about?" He still wore the cloth around his waist, his chest bare and damp from his hot shower and looking oh so good.

He sat down beside her, his big body seeming to tower over hers as he looked down at her. "I thought maybe we could talk about what happened, you know, with Iteena." She swallowed again, his intoxicating scent enveloping her and making her brain malfunction.

"Okay." The word was spoken deeply, yet tentatively.

"I shouldn't have reacted like I did. I miss you, a lot, and well, you were honest with me. Maybe it wasn't from the very beginning, but you were still honest. I'd like to start over, put this whole situation behind us. Can we do that, just forget about it?" She reached her hand out and put it over his. He looked down at their hands, his body still tightly coiled but slowly loosening up.

"I'd like to start over. I've missed you so much, *fallina*. I'm sorry, so very sorry."

She looked into his strong warrior face and smiled, bringing her hand up and running it over his cheek. He closed his eyes leaned into her touch. She moved closer to him, his eyes opening and their gazes locked. He leaned in also, his movements slow and tentative as he pressed his lips to her forehead and slowly moving down to her lips. She welcomed the kiss and opened her mouth to let his tongue slide in. They lay down, facing each other as their mouths continued their slow exploration. She moved her hands along the hard, defined contours of his body, becoming wetter with each slide against his still damp flesh.

His hand slid down her shoulder and arm, over the dip of her waist and hips until it stopped on her upper thigh. He slid her dress up until it rested on her waist and lifted her leg over his own. Cool air wafted across her pussy and her skin formed goose bumps as his hand continued to move over her exposed flesh. She speared her hand through his hair and brought his mouth closer, needing to have him as close to her body as possible. He groaned and she swallowed it, loving the idea that he was just as worked up as her.

He gripped her hip and pulled her on top of him, sliding her dress up and over her head and throwing to the floor. She looked down at him and ran her hands over the smooth planes of his chest, around his stiff copper colored nipples, and down the rolling hills of his abdomen. The cloth around his waist had fallen open and his erection lay against his abdomen, hard and ready. The head of his shaft reached past his belly button, making her pussy clench with an almost desperate need. She grabbed his cock and lifted her hips up, sliding the head along the folds of her vagina, and gathering the moisture he had caused. She placed the tip at the mouth of her pussy, her hole widening around his cock head until it slid all the way in. He gripped her thighs and groaned, his green eyes seeming to glow in the darkness.

"Go slow, *fallina*. I want to feel your pussy walls all around me—want to savor this moment."

She rested her hands on his pecs and slowly went down on him, her vagina stretching all around his huge cock until she rested on his pelvis. She let her head fall back and moaned out in bliss, the feeling of being completely filled overpowering her senses.

"Oh, yes. Ride me nice…and…slow."

She lifted up slowly, the head of his cock almost slipping out before she slid back down on him again. She leaned back and rested her hands on his thighs, lifting her hips up and down, squeezing her eyes closed as pleasure coursed through her. He pumped his hips up as she lowered her pussy down on him. The rhythm was smooth and steady, a perfect union of their bodies. Her nipples tightened into hard beads and her pussy became slick with need. His thumb moved to her clit and rubbed it in a slow circle as his other hand gripped an aching nipple and lightly pinched it. Soon, sweat coated their bodies as they both moved up and down, the pleasure becoming almost unbearable. She lifted up and then slammed back down again, over and over until her climax peaked and exploded inside of her.

    She moaned loudly as his thighs tensed beneath her and his moan matched her own. She felt the tip of his cock touch her cervix, the hot jets of his semen shooting deep into her womb. Her orgasm went on and on until she was clenched so hard on him the pleasure and pain became one. Both of his fingers pulled and plucked at her nipples as his thrusting hips didn't let up. She continued to move her pussy up and down his shaft, determined to wring every last drop of his cum out.

    She fell forward, their sweat-slicked bodies moving sensuously together with every breath they took. He rolled her onto her back and covered her body with his own, his cock still hard and pulsing inside of her. She wrapped her legs around his waist and closed her eyes as her pleasure mounted again. He licked and kissed her collar bone, dragging his tongue up her neck and claiming her mouth. His tongue slipped inside of hers, stroking and sliding over every inch that he could reach. Her clit rubbed against his skin, his cock moving at a fast and slick rhythm inside of her that had her second orgasm coming on strong.

    She gripped his shoulders, her nails biting into his flesh as white-hot pleasure streaked through her. He ate up her scream, his hips pounding harder into her until she felt his second orgasm coat her walls. Her pussy clenched and unclenched around his shaft, her body so sensitive every cell in her body was alive with pleasure. He tensed and groaned one last time before his body sagged on top of hers. His muscular body made her very aware of how feminine she was. He pulled up and stared down at her, love shining back at her as he kissed her on the forehead.

"I love you so much."

"I love you, Keirak." He rolled off of her and brought her close to him, pulling the blankets over them and wrapping his arms around her. She curled into him, the feeling of love and protectiveness surrounding her and making sleep come easy.

Chapter Fourteen

Icezak sat in the dining chamber, his complete attention on Kalina who sat with the other females she had come with. When he learned her tribe had been slaughtered and that she was harmed, he had been furious—still was. Just thinking about it made his blood heat and his anger rise.

She wore a non-transparent gown, something that pleased him. He continuously reminded himself she was much too young for him, but every time he looked at her womanly curves and her soft features, it made his cock grow unbearably hard. She did a good job of not noticing him, but he sure as hell noticed her. Her black hair was piled high on her head and showed off her creamy, slender neck, the deep dip of the gown showing off the perfectly rounded swells of her breasts. He swallowed, his throat instantly going dry. She would be staying with the tribe, and he knew it would be the worst kind of hell. He wanted her desperately, but she was something he could never have. She was a royal and an innocent, much too good for him—a warrior who killed everyday.

He could smell her sorrow all the way across the room, a scent so fresh and clean it made his heart ache. As much as he physically desired her, there was something else inside of him that had nothing to do with getting her naked. He had the urge to comfort her, speak to her, and let her know everything would be okay. The emotions were foreign to him, feelings he had no idea how to handle. He should speak to her, give her his condolences and let her know he was there for her. He shook his head, knowing a female of worth like her would never want a roughened warrior like him. He looked down and moved his food, his appetite suddenly disappearing.

* * * *

Kitty headed over to the garden, wanting to pick some fresh flowers for Mena and the children but really just missing the intoxicating fragrance that surrounded the room. She stopped in the doorway, her throat closing tight as she saw flaming red hair and a curvy body. Iteena turned around, a smile on her face as she stepped forward.

"Hello."

Kitty stared at her, shocked that Iteena spoke English. She didn't want to be rude, but then again, this was the same woman who knowingly tried to seduce Keirak even though she knew he was taken.

"Hi." Kitty spoke the word quietly, walking into the room and starting to pick flowers. She kept her back toward Iteena, feeling the woman come up behind her. Her presence was strong and a feeling of unease settled inside of Kitty.

"I really am sorry for all the trouble I caused. I would like to offer my apologies."

Kitty turned around and stared into brown eyes that seemed so flat and emotionless it gave her chills. She wore a dress that was really just strips of cloth wrapped around her body, her breasts and vagina clearly visible through the material. She came off pleasant and sincere, but Kitty sensed something deep down, something that lurked below the surface.

"You speak English very well. Where did you learn it?"

She shrugged and examined her nails. "My tribe spoke many languages. Do you come here a lot?" She gestured around the room, a smile on her full lips and her white teeth flashing.

"Yes." Something in the back of her mind told her to lie, but she pushed it away knowing it was probably her jealousy from how things had played out.

"This place is quite beautiful."

Kitty turned back around and picked more flowers, trying her hardest to ignore Iteena's menacing presence.

"Well, I better go. I just saw this room and stopped in. I'm sure we'll see each other later."

She didn't turn around or respond and instantly felt like a bitch. For all she knew, Iteena was sincere in her apology. She blew out a breath and turned around, about to call her back but she was already gone. She didn't know how long Iteena or the other three females planned on staying, but she might as well get over it and get along with her.

* * * *

Kitty held a bouquet of flowers in her hand and made her way toward the hot springs where she knew Mena would be. It had quickly become Mena's favorite cavern, and Kitty didn't blame her. Her attention was on the flowers and she didn't realize someone had stepped into the hallway with her until they brushed their fingers along her shoulder. She spun around, so startled she lost her footing and twisted her ankle. Before she hit the ground, strong arms grabbed her waist and lifted her up. She stared with wide eyed at Rhyson. A smile covered his lips as his eyes stared at her breasts. "Excuse me." Her words were short and clipped and she struggled out of his grip, wincing when she put weight on her tender ankle.

"You have hurt yourself. Would you like me to carry you back to your room?"

He wrapped his arms around her waist and brought her close again, lifting her easily so that she dangled off the ground. "Let go of me, Rhyson."

He chuckled and brought his head to her hair and inhaled deeply. "I can see what the appeal is—you smell intoxicating."

"Thatukka mehatha vadom."

Keirak's voice speared through the hallway, all deep and rough and sending shivers down her spine. She turned her head, her smile faltering when she saw the look that covered his handsome features. His body tense and his jaw clenched as his eyes stayed on Rhyson.

"Such harsh words. I was only teasing your mate." Rhyson set her down and took a step back, his hands going up and his palms facing outward in surrender.

"Apologize to *my* mate."

She swallowed and took a few steps toward Keirak, wincing every time she put pressure on her ankle. Keirak was by her in the next instance, his arms scooping her up and cradling to his chest as he gripped her tight.

"You will apologize for your dishonorable behavior, Rhyson."

"It's okay, let's just go." The tension was getting so thick in the small quarters it was starting to suffocate her.

"No, he *will* apologize to you *now*."

Keirak's complete attention was on Rhyson, his jaw still tense as she heard him grind his teeth. She could see the anger practically radiating off of him and stole a quick glance toward Rhyson who looked just like Keirak. A power play went on, but ultimately Rhyson obeyed Keirak—the second in command.

"As you wish. I apologize. Do you accept?"

She nodded her head and whispered for Keirak to just leave. She blew out a relieved breath when he did just that. He kissed the top of her head and headed toward their room. She looked back at Rhyson, his body in the same spot, his fists clenching and unclenching as he stared at the ground. The flowers would just have to wait for another day because she wasn't going back there now. Rhyson didn't frighten her, she knew no one in the tribe would harm her, but there was something off about him, something dangerous that made her want to tread lightly around him.

"You need to be careful around him. Rhyson can be unstable at times, and I don't want you to inadvertently get injured. Promise me you will stay away from him."

"I promise." She had no intentions of going near him. "He just always seems to be there."

"I know, *fallina*, but the next time I won't be so lenient with him."

Chapter Fifteen

The next day, Kitty took the flowers she picked the day before and headed over to Mena's room. Last night, Keirak had taken her fast and hard, his possessiveness clear in the way he fucked her, and he definitely fucked her. She still had the smile to prove it, and her body was still deliciously sore. She walked nice and slow, her ankle still bothering her but not as bad.

"Hello."

Kitty stopped and looked over her shoulder, forcing herself to play nice. Iteena sauntered up to her, so close she could see the individual red eyelashes on the woman. "Hi." She turned fully around, straightening her back and pasting on a smile. She still didn't feel right about her, but she made herself act normal.

"Will you come with me to the garden room? I want to pick some flowers for the girls but don't know which ones will be the best."

Kitty shook her head and held up her own flowers. "I can't right now. I have to give these to someone, maybe later though."

"Please." Iteena held out on the last syllable and held her hands out in a pleading motion. "It'll only take a moment, I promise."

Kitty breathed out, nodded reluctantly, and followed her to the garden. Once they entered, Kitty made fast, sure work of showing Iteena the most beautiful and exotic ones. She started to leave and stopped when Iteena grabbed her arm.

"Are you sure these are all the right ones?"

Kitty looked down at where the woman's nails gripped her arm, her nails painted a bright red and the points like claws. "Yeah, those are fine." Just as she was about to rip her arm free when shouts and war cries broke through the air.

"Right on schedule."

Kitty watched the whole thing in slow motion—Iteena's hand curling into a fist, rearing back, and coming straight toward her face. The movements were so quick, Kitty didn't have time to move away. Iteena's fist slammed into her face, knocking her sideways and causing her body to spin around before hitting the ground. She opened her eyes, the room spinning as she looked into the hallway and saw several boots coming toward her. She tried to sit up but that only caused her to get kicked in the ribs and fall back down. Iteena's bare feet came into her view, her toenails painted the same bright red as her fingernails.

"You know, he would have tired of you sooner than later. Keirak and I have a long history together, and you're just in the way."

Kitty cried out in pain as she was pulled up by a chunk of her hair. Kitty gasped as she brought her eyes up to the men that stood in front of her. They were big and tall, war paint covering all of their faces except for one—the one with a scarred face. Iteena let go of her hair and shoved her forward.

"This is the one that needs to be gone. I don't care what you do with her just as long as I don't have to look at her face."

"Kikttak-oo-thae broodthek."

"Speak in her language. I want her to know exactly what you plan on doing to her."

Kitty looked with wide eyes between Iteena and the giant in front of her, his scar so pronounced on his face it only added to her fright. "What's going on? Why are you doing this?" She winced in pain as the beast in front of her slapped her so hard she tasted blood. *Where's Keirak?* War cries still sounded in the distance as well as screams and shouts.

"You do not speak until you are spoken to, female."

Kitty held her cheek as he walked around her, his finger trailing over her skin, disgust filling her.

"I think I might keep you for myself, although, I don't know if your body is strong enough to handle my more…aggressive appetites. Makes no difference though, we'll soon break that sweet little body of yours in." He ran a finger down her cheek, making her cringe away. "And how is my fair daughter this eve?"

Daughter? Kitty looked between the two of them, their appearances completely opposite, but the evil inside of them the same. She grew sicker and sicker by the minute, this whole situation becoming a nightmare. Iteena walked up and gave her father a hug, turning and looking at Kitty with a sadistic smile on her face.

"Now don't look at us that way. If you had just stayed away from Keirak, I would have spared your life, but you had to go after him."

Kitty kept her mouth shut because she knew that saying something would just end up causing her a lot of pain. She dropped her head, feeling the hot tears slide down her face and fall to the floor.

"Let's move out."

The scarred one grabbed her arm hard enough to leave a bruise and pushed her toward the front. She acted as his shield, leading the way like a dog on a leash. When they rounded the last corner that led into the main cave, she stopped. Men fought against each other, ZorZacks and strangers, each of them equal in size. She spotted Keirak immediately, blood covering his body, but she couldn't see any new wounds.

Every man he fought dropped to the ground within seconds before he moved to the next. Rhyson stood on the opposite side, the serpent tattoo on his body moving over his skin as if it were alive. His eyes glowed silver, swirling and shining bright and making him look fiercer—more frightening. She looked back at Keirak, his eyes on her and his face turning red with anger.

He stormed toward her, knocking down anyone who got in his way with just a slash of his sword. She was pulled back and thrown down on the ground, the breath getting knocked out of her as she landed hard. She stared up with wide eyes as Keirak and the scarred one stepped toe-to-toe. The scarred one smirked and showed a set of brownish teeth as a look of horror covered Keirak's features. They started to speak in a language she couldn't understand, the scarred one laughing as Keirak shouted angry words at him.

"Isn't this a happy reunion, my father and my lover meeting again after so many years."

She ignored Iteena's upbeat words, her voice sounding cheery as she stared at Keirak with longing in her eyes.

"Want to know a little secret?" Iteena didn't wait for a reply. "My father killed Keirak's tribe years ago."

Kitty looked into her face with horror and remembered Keirak's story about the tribe leader who killed his family—the one with the scarred face.

"You don't look that surprised. Such a shame, I so do love to see the look of shock across people's faces."

The men who stood behind the scarred one, stepped forward, immediately stopping when their leaders hand shot up for them to be still. Fighting continued all around them— grunts and curses ringing throughout the cavern.

* * * *

Keirak stared into the face of the male he hated most—the male that took his family, his tribe from him. He had hunted him down for years with no success, but here he stood, mere feet away, daring to take his love. The scarred rogue looked much the same he did all those years ago, only minimal signs of aging showing on his hardened face.

"You are much fiercer now that you are a man, but what makes you think you will be able to save your beloved when you couldn't even save your tribe?"

Keirak fisted his hands, wanting to strike the male before him but reining his temper in. He took a step toward Kitty, a male stepping right next to her and pulling a blade out. "You touch her and you're as good as dead."

"You would do well to keep back unless you want her headless. We have a score to settle. Your female is only minimally harmed, but I guarantee if you move one more step toward her, I'll have her neck sliced clean open."

Keirak kept flicking his eyes toward Kitty, her lip split open and a black eye forming. He gritted his teeth at her state, wanting nothing more than to tear this males body parts off of him slowly and painfully. He believed the words the rogue spoke, why would he doubt them? This is the same male, the same tribe that slaughtered his family right into front of him. "I am no longer a child that you can toss to the side. Won't you fight me now that we are the same?" Keirak taunted him, and by the way the scarred males face became red, it was doing its job.

The rogues stepped back, giving Keirak and their leader the room they needed to finish this once and for all. Just as Keirak took the first step forward, Iteena darted out and ran up to the scarred male. "No, don't!" Keirak shouted and held his hand out, not wanting her to get harmed by his enemy. His mouth dropped open as she laid her hands on the leader's chest and spoke fast words—pleading words to who she called "father." "What is the meaning of this?"

She turned around and took a step toward him as tears ran down her face. "Let's just leave, Keirak, just run away together. My father will let you go unharmed if you just back down now. I can make you so happy, *we* can be so happy together. Won't you leave with me now?"

He shook his head, confusion and anger coursing through him as he watched her—the traitor. "You brought them here? Why?"

"It wasn't my intention, but then she got in the way." Iteena stabbed a finger at Kitty, venom dripping from each word. "I had to get rid of her so that we can finally be together."

"This is the male you want—this worthless piece of hide that cowered before me so many years ago? I think not, daughter, you will step away *now*."

He looked over at Kitty who watched him with wide eyes, tears streaming down her cheeks as she mouthed, "I love you." She was his life, his soul and his heart—his future.

He turned back around, vaguely aware that Iteena pleaded with the enemy, but he didn't focus on her, he kept his eyes trained on the male before him, knowing that one wrong move would result in Kitty's death. In the next instant, Keirak was tackled to the ground, a fist slamming into the side of his head and not letting up. He shoved the heavy weight off of him, the body flying in the air and slamming against the rock wall. A female scream cut through the air—Iteena's screech like glass in his ears. He pulled himself off the ground and stalked forward, his fists clenched tight and burning to hit something. "You know, I never did catch the name of the male I'm about to kill."

The rouge leader laughed and spit blood onto the dirt floor. "It's Helix, but I only tell you so that you know whose hands you will die by."

They crashed together, a tangle of limbs in the center of the circle. Keirak slammed his fist into Helix's nose, blood spraying out like a waterfall as Helix howled in pain. Keirak felt a sharp pain in his side and knew he had been stabbed. They stumbled back, Helix gripping his nose as blood continued to pour down his face and splash against the dirt covered floor. Keirak brought his hand down to his wound, blood covering his skin as he looked back at the rogue. Helix's face turned into a mask of rage, his meaty fists raised high as he lunged forward. They fell backward, both of them trying to get the upper hand and have dominance over the fight.

Keirak grabbed Helix's arm and gave a quick twist, the bone breaking in two easily. Helix howled in pain, his arm hanging limply at an odd angle. In a quick move, Keirak unsheathed his sword strapped to his back, and swung it in a wide arch before pushing it forward and sliding it into Helix's abdomen. The blade went in easily, and he twisted the blade, making the wound bigger and more painful. He pulled the sword out and stepped back, breathing heavily but keeping his eyes trained ahead of him. Helix fell back, gripping the wound as blood poured out of it. Iteena rushed forward, falling to her knees and screaming out. Keirak fell to the ground, his knees hitting the hard surface as he sucked in air.

Helix lay on ground, blood coming out of his mouth as he stared at the ceiling with a blank look covering his features. Keirak suddenly felt so dizzy, the room moving in every direction as blood seeped out of his wound. He fell to his hands, needing to get to Kitty but the act seeming too difficult. He attempted to stand but stumbled back down, his eyes growing heavy as the room slowly went black.

* * * *

Kitty gasped as Keirak fell to the ground. Her breath caught and her heart hurting as she stood up. Men fought fiercely all around her, the sounds of their weapons slamming together deafening. She rushed forward, heedless of the fighting, her only objective—get to Keirak. Everything became hazy as she fell to her knees next to Keirak. Tears fell from her eyes and she squeezed them shut as pain overtook her. She opened her eyes and looked down at him. He looked so pale and his skin was so cold that she feared he was already dead. She dropped her head to his chest, desperate to hear his heartbeat. She started to weep hard when she heard the soft but steady rhythm. She quickly tore off a piece of her dress and wadded the material against his bleeding wound. He grunted and slowly fluttered his eyes open, smiling as he stared up at her.

Soon, the deafening noise in the room became softer, more bodies falling to the ground, but only those of the ZorZack enemy. She ran her hand over his cheek and smiled at him, tears falling from her eyes and landing on his bare skin. She looked up and stared at Iteena who continued to weep over her father. Kitty felt no remorse for the female who had brought all of this trouble. As Kitty stared at her, Iteena suddenly stopped crying and turned her head to stare at her. There was such unadulterated hate pouring off of that look that Kitty felt it all the way to her bones. Iteena slowly rose and turned so that she faced Kitty, her body tense as she took a step forward.

"You are the reason my father is dead! You are the reason Keirak is injured! If it wasn't for you, none of this would have happened!"

She screamed and ran toward her, her claw-like nails curled and clearly her weapon of choice. Kitty stumbled back, her hand bumping Keirak's sword before she instinctively grabbed it and lifted the massive weight forward. Iteena continued to rush forward, the blade slipping into her chest like a knife through a slab of meat. Kitty gagged at the sensation but kept it upright as Iteena's eyes went wide and she gasped. Gravity pushed her down on the blade until her open-mouthed face was inches from Kitty's.

Kitty was vaguely aware of Keirak shouting and his hand brushing against her body. She couldn't afford to take her attention off of Iteena, and blocked out everything but her and the other woman. Iteena was gurgling, blood slowly coming out as she opened and closed her mouth. Tears streamed down Kitty's cheeks as Iteena's eyes slowly closed and her last breath left her lips. She didn't move until her arms started to protest the weight. She dropped the sword, the body attached to it hitting the ground with a sickening thud. She crawled over to Keirak, crying harder as she laid her head on his chest.

She leaned against him long enough that the wetness on her cheeks dried. She pulled back and looked into Keirak's face, love and compassion etched into his features as he stroked her cheek.

"My love."

His words were spoken softly as his lips brushed gently against hers. Just as she was about to pull away, the air around her became thick. The hairs on her arms stood up and she gasped and pulled away. She looked around, the wall off to her side starting to waver right in front of her. The warriors moved away from the hazy wall as it started to swirl and change color. A loud whooshing noise filled the room, and she knew exactly why that noise sounded so familiar. It was the same noise that had greeted her when she first saw the portal—the portal that had brought her and Mena into Dimi of the Seven Moons. The greens, blues, and whites swirled together, and she looked at Keirak. He wasn't staring at the portal—he was staring right at her, fear clearly covering his face.

"Keirak?" He didn't speak, just continued to stare at her. She broke the eye contact and looked again at the portal. It was her way home—her escape so that she could go back to everything and everyone she knew. She turned her head and saw Mena standing beside Demariak, Cayllum in her arms and Nea in his. Mena stared at Kitty, her eyebrows bunched and worry covering her face. Kitty turned again and stared at Keirak before she stood. She noticed everyone step away from her, the tension in the room so thick it was hard to breathe. *Isn't this what you have been waiting for? To go back home to everything that you miss?*

She looked at Mena again, and then to Cayllum, Demariak, and little Nea. She loved them all like they were her family. She looked at Keirak who was now sitting up, his hand pressed against his side as he watched her with concern. She loved him so much. She looked at the portal once more, knowing that she needed to do what was right, what she felt was right in her heart. She turned and dropped to her knees in front of Keirak, framing his face as tears ran down her cheeks. "I love you."

"Are you saying goodbye?" His voice was rough, his jaw clenched tight and his eyes set hard.

She kissed him gently. "Yes, this is goodbye." His eyes grew big before his face took on that stern look she loved so much. She smoothed her finger along the crease between his eyes, smiling softly as she brought her lips to his again. "This is goodbye to my old life. I want to stay here with you, with my family." She looked over and Mena and smiled, tears running down her best friends face as Demariak smiled and clutched his wife closer. This was her new life, the life she had been waiting for but had yet to see. Keirak was the one she loved, and it took her this long to realize that it didn't matter where she was, she was surrounded by whom and what she needed in her life. How could she turn away from that?

Epilogue

Kitty sat on the bed, baby Cayllum lying between her legs as he slept. Nea lay on her other side, the little girl sound asleep and lightly snoring. She felt Keirak's arm wrap around her shoulder and she turned and smiled up at him. He sat next to him, a bandage covering his wounds and bruises marring his golden skin. She was watching the children tonight while Mena and Demariak had some much needed alone time. Keirak leaned down and brought his lips toward hers, the kiss so gentle and sweet it made her heart warm and swell with happiness and love.

Cayllum started to squirm and whimper and she quickly picked him up, cradling him to her chest and rocking him back and forth. She ran her finger over his tiny dark eyebrows, a small smile playing over his bow like mouth as he drifted back to sleep.

"I want this for you, *fallina*. I want this for *us*."

"What? Babysitting?" He chuckled and kissed her on the top of the head. His love surrounded her, an actual power that was filled with electricity and went right through her.

"I mean, I want you to be a mother. I want to have a family with you, if you want that, too."

She looked into his bright green eyes. She had never really thought about motherhood, but as she held the small bundle in her arms, and had her powerful and fierce warrior beside her, she knew that she truly did want this. She looked over at Nea, the little girl's face relaxed and so innocent as she slept. "I want a family, but more importantly, I want that family with you." She looked over at him and brought her lips to his, putting all the love she felt for him into the kiss. Her life had changed so dramatically, and even though she had wanted to leave this entire world behind, she couldn't even dream of it now. This was her home, and Keirak was her life. She couldn't be happier.

THE END

http://www.JenikaSnow.com

ABOUT THE AUTHOR

Jenika is just your average woman. She lives in the too hot northeast with her husband and their young daughter. Thankfully, her husband shares her unusual sense of humor and naughty nature.

Along with taking care of their daughter, they have to keep an eye on Milo and Ottis, their spunky cats. When not writing, Jenika works full-time at a hospital and attends nursing school. Writing is Jenika's number one passion, but since life gets in the way, she isn't able to write full-time (at least not yet.)

Jenika started writing at a very young age. Her first story consisted of a young girl who traveled to an exotic island and found a magical doll. That story has long since disappeared, but her passion for writing has stayed strong.

Jenika loves to hear from readers, and encourages them to contact her and give their feedback.

Also by Jenika Snow

Siren Classic: *The Chosen: A Tale of the Blood Breed*
Siren Classic: *Blush: A Story of Dominance and Submission*
Ménage Amour: *Lilly's Surrender*

Available at
BOOKSTRAND.COM

Siren Publishing, Inc.
www.SirenPublishing.com

LaVergne, TN USA
10 April 2011
223644LV00006B/37/P